WHO PLANTED THE BODY?

"Get over here!" Ruth's voice screeched in Helma's ear. "Hurry up."

Helma stood beside her bed, barefoot, fresh from her shower. Water dripped from her hair down the center of her back. What was startling was that it was only six-thirty in the morning. Ruth rarely got out of bed before ten o'clock, a habit Helma found unhealthy and completely dismaying.

"Ruth, you're screaming," Helma said calmly.

Ruth panted as if she couldn't catch her breath. "You would be too. Get over here. I've . . . He's . . . Helma Zukas," Ruth said in careful enunciation. "Are you familiar with the periwinkle that grows next to my garage?"

"Yes. Is it blooming?"

"At this moment, there's a man lying in it. And he's D-E-A-D!"

MISS ZUKAS
❧ AND THE ❧
STROKE OF DEATH

JO DERESKE

AVON

TWILIGHT

AVON BOOKS, INC.
1350 Avenue of the Americas
New York, New York 10019

Copyright © 1995 by Jo Dereske
Published by arrangement with the author
Library of Congress Catalog Card Number: 95-94489
ISBN: 0-380-77033-4
www.avonbooks.com/twilight

First Avon Twilight Printing: March 1999
First Avon Books Printing: December 1995

AVON TWILIGHT TRADEMARK REG. U.S. PAT. OFF. AND IN OTHER COUNTRIES,
MARCA REGISTRADA, HECHO EN U.S.A.

Printed in the U.S.A.

WCD 10 9 8 7 6 5 4 3 2

For K. and the nephews

Acknowledgments

The "Snow to Surf" Race in this book is loosely based on the annual Ski to Sea Race in Whatcom County, Washington, a torturous eighty-five-mile relay race from the 4,300-foot level of Mount Baker to Bellingham Bay during a seven-to-eleven-hour period every Memorial Day weekend. The race is internationally known for its tough course, good sportsmanship, and the nine hundred volunteers who make it happen.

CONTENTS

CONTENTS

CONTENTS

❦ chapter one ❦

SUDDEN DEATH

On Wednesday evening, when Binky died, Miss Helma Zukas had remained late at the Bellehaven Public Library, struggling to compose a persuasive memo to Ms. Moon, the library director, regarding Ms. Moon's newest scheme: to hold overnight "camp-outs" for grade-schoolers in the library building.

Other than her pale blue computer screen, Helma Zukas's desk lamp was the only illumination in the cramped library workroom. She'd turned off the buzzing fluorescent tubes overhead and now the room settled broodingly around Helma's blue-lit cubicle as the evening lengthened.

Beyond the closed workroom door, the public still used the library but the workroom itself had been deserted for hours, providing a perfect place for endeavors that required intense concentration. Helma backspaced, obliterated the word "lunacy," and swiftly replaced it with "injudicious."

"I read they hold 'camp-outs' in the Denver Museum of Natural History with great success," Ms. Moon had said at yesterday's staff meeting, her blue eyes fervently wide and distantly focused. "It gives children the feeling of ownership of the facility."

Helma didn't bother to point out that Bellehaven,

Washington was hardly Denver, Colorado—thankfully. Although she did mention that giving ten-year-olds the illusion they owned the Bellehaven Public Library might not exactly be to the library's advantage.

A stealthy rustle like the gentle crumpling of paper came from the small staff lounge at the rear of the workroom. Helma ignored it, wondering briefly if Eve had left the cookies out again and whether Jack the janitor had remembered to set another mousetrap.

George Melville, the catalog librarian who staffed the reference desk on Wednesday evenings, opened the door and stuck his bearded head inside the workroom. A triangle of light from the public area illuminated his thinning hair and cast disproportionate shadows across the walls.

"Buttoning this place up in five minutes, Helma," George said. "Time for all good librarians to head home and recharge for another exciting day in the information trenches."

"Thank you," Helma said, glancing at her watch and noting the disturbing way that time evaporated when she concentrated, especially when a computer was involved.

"What are you working on?" George asked.

"A memo about the camp-outs."

George laughed. "I don't believe you've heard the whole sordid story yet."

"What do you mean?" Helma asked. Behind George, a woman carrying a stack of books squinted into the workroom over his shoulder.

"There's another devilish component to the Moonbeam's plan. Only rumors so far and I know how you hate rumors so I won't bore you with them." He wagged his fingers at Helma and shook his head. "Wait'll you hear! Ta-ta."

Helma returned to her computer screen, doubting Ms. Moon could have anything more farfetched up her sleeve than flocks of children bedded down in the middle of library stacks. She pushed F-10 to save her memo, exited her word processing program, and flicked off her computer, hoping a night's sleep would provide her with further argument. It frequently did.

As she pulled out of the staff parking lot, Miss Zukas pretended not to see George Melville pushing his bicycle, headlight shining, rear lights blinking, from the bookmobile entrance where he hid it on nights he worked. Reflector strips criss-crossed his helmet and pedals, yellow lights were strapped to his calves. George's doctor had ordered more exercise, Roberta, the genealogy librarian, had confided to the whole staff, and this was George's response. He only rode his bicycle after dark because—again from Roberta—"he's embarrassed by the size of his bum."

Helma drove her Buick two miles over the speed limit along the shore of Washington Bay toward her apartment in the Bayside Arms. Traffic on the boulevard was sparse. It was too early in the year for tourists, too late in the evening for sunset watchers. A few lights twinkled across Washington Bay, the water between a crescent of darkness.

It was Miss Zukas's sixteenth spring in Bellehaven, Washington, sixteen years since she'd left Michigan for her first professional library job and still she couldn't take for granted the mountains and islands, the temperate climate, and the verdant growth. It was cold, as it usually was on an April evening in Bellehaven, but Helma rolled down her window two inches and let the fragrance of sea water and spring growth blow into her car.

The clouds had cleared off that afternoon and as Helma walked across the parking lot to the Bayside Arms she paused to study the night sky where she knew the starry outline of Ursa Major was located. But the lights of Bellehaven were too bright to see the constellation.

Helma's apartment was on the third floor of the Bayside Arms, accessible by a flight of outside stairs or an elevator Helma had never ridden. Even when Helma moved into the Bayside Arms sixteen years ago, she'd lugged her belongings up three flights of stairs rather than ride the elevator.

By the light over her door Helma noted that for the second time in a week the *Bellehaven Daily News* had been properly inserted into the newspaper tube beside her apartment door. She nodded in approval and tucked it beneath her arm while she unlocked the door to apartment 3F, pausing on the threshold to ascertain everything was in order. Helma Zukas had a sense about order and disorder, able to detect the latter, even in the chaotic belongings of others.

But no, her apartment was exactly as she'd left it: kitchen spotless, living room tidily in place, drapes pulled.

As she hung her coat in her coat closet, buttoning the top button to keep it straight on the hanger, an irritated meow sounded from the small balcony that jutted from the rear of the building, facing the wide scoop of Washington Bay. Boy Cat Zukas stared balefully in through the two inches of unshaded space she left at the bottom of her balcony door. It was as close as she allowed him to the interior of her apartment.

Helma Zukas did not own Boy Cat Zukas. She'd never had an interest in owning a cat and, in fact, felt a quiver of unease at any feline sighting, whether it was a fuzzy kitten or a sleek leopard in a zoo, similar to what many people felt at being surprised by a snake slithering across their path. Because she'd had no choice a year ago but to save Boy Cat Zukas from certain death, he assumed something akin to a relationship between them. Helma did not.

She fed him to discourage him from leaving bird wings and mouse heads on her balcony and kept a basket holding an old pillow in the balcony corner to dissuade him from sleeping in her potted flowers. Each morning she opened her drapes in a vain hope he'd disappeared during the night. If Helma chose to sit on her balcony, she firmly encouraged Boy Cat Zukas to vacate.

Helma's doorbell rang as she ran water into her tea kettle. Through the peephole, Helma recognized Walter David, the manager of Bayside Arms. She sighed, wondering what he wanted *this* time. Howard Marble, the old manager, had never bothered his tenants as often as Walter David did.

"Yes?" Helma asked, opening her door partway.

Walter David tugged the brim of his Seattle Mariners cap and smiled, exposing a gold filling behind his left canine. He wore a black leather motorcycle jacket over a "Just Did It" t-shirt and Levis with faded and frayed knees. Helma suspected she and Walter David were the same age, both in their late thirties, only she was certain he showed the wear of his years far more than she did.

"How are you, Miss Zukas?"

"I'm fine. Thank you."

"That's good. Me too. Fine, that is." Walter David's voice dwindled off to silence and still he stood on the coco mat in front of her door, smiling.

"Is there apartment business we need to discuss?" Helma asked.

"No. I mean, yes. I wondered if you received your newspaper all right."

Behind Helma, her phone rang.

"You can get that if you want," Walter David offered, making a move to step inside her apartment. "I'll wait."

"The telephone can wait," Helma said, standing firm and opting for the choice with the least potential entanglements.

Walter David's smile widened. "So the paper was in your paper holder?"

"Yes, it was," Helma said between the third and fourth ring.

"Good. I personally told the paper boy: no more tossing. Gotta put them where they belong. That's what those paper tubes are for. 'Get it right every night,' I said."

"I appreciate that."

The phone quit after the seventh ring.

Walter David nodded and asked, "Do you like motorcycles?"

"I haven't thought about them in years," Helma told him, seeing a quick vision of her father and Uncle Tony roaring off deer hunting on Uncle Tony's Moto Guzzi one November morning in Michigan before the snows came, their rifles slung behind them like cowboys.

"Would you like to go for a ride someday?"

"I've never . . ."

"I'm really good." Walter David flushed. "On a bike. Driving, I mean."

Helma had seen him careen into the manager's parking space, dwarfed by his oversized rumbling motorcycle with the buxom redhead painted on the gas tank and the homemade box in which he sometimes carried his Persian cat. "I'm not certain . . ."

Walter David brushed her words aside. "When the weather's nicer, I mean. Wind's still pretty cold. You think about it." He flashed gold at her again. "See ya. Call me if the paper doesn't make it."

Helma closed and locked the door and drew the deadbolt, glancing at the silent phone, wondering who had called.

And that was how she missed learning of Binky's death until the following morning.

❧ chapter two ❧

CIRCLES OF HARMONY

Helma steered her Buick into her parking space beside the Bellehaven Public Library, leaning to the right slightly and closing one eye to line up the Buick's hood ornament with the flagpole on the library lawn—assuring she was equidistant from the yellow borders of the parking space—and turned off the engine.

The staff was gathered in the small lounge at the end of the workroom. When Eve Oxnard, the fiction librarian, saw Helma enter, she waved a half-eaten cookie, beckoning Helma to join them. Helma Zukas, who rarely made exaggerated arm motions inside buildings, nodded, concealing a grimace when she saw the cookie in Eve's hand, wondering if the box of cookies *had* sat out all night, and if that *had* been a mouse rustling in the box the night before.

But first, Helma stowed her purse in her desk drawer, hung up her coat, and checked her lipstick in the mirror she kept beside her paper clip holder. Glancing over the shelves that separated her cubicle from Patrice's, she noticed that Patrice, the social science librarian, hadn't arrived yet, which was unusual. Patrice preferred to be the first one in the building so she could, Helma suspected, keep an eye on who did what, hoarding her observations like captured ammunition for future battles.

For years Patrice had threatened to claim her retirement and relocate to the Southwest, "where the sun shines all day," but each time it came down to an irrevocable decision, Patrice postponed filing the paperwork until 'later.'

George Melville, the cataloger, Mrs. Carmon, the circulation clerk, Roberta Seymour, the Washington history and genealogy librarian, and Eve turned solemn faces to Helma as she entered the lounge.

Something had happened. Helma felt a sizzling shiver at the base of her neck, all her senses eagerly awakening, her surroundings becoming distinct and charged with potency.

Coffee dripped into the coffee pot. Staff cups gleamed from their hooks. Ms. Moon had changed the saying on the wall over the coffee machine to "Keep your eyes on the stars." The quote had an unfinished feel, as if Ms. Moon had edited it. Helma stored the phrase in the back of her mind to look up later.

"Did you hear?" Mrs. Carmon asked, her voice dulcet with sorrow. "Did she call you? It's so sad." Mrs. Carmon removed her bifocals and dabbed her eyes with a pink tissue.

"A tragedy," George Melville said, eyeing the box of cookies, one eyebrow raised in an expression Helma recognized as not exactly connoting tragedy.

Helma didn't drink coffee; she preferred tea. She poured hot water over a tea bag nestled inside a cup illustrated with elephants engaged in mysterious activities. It wasn't a cup she'd have purchased for herself but she used it at the library because it was a gift from her favorite nephew.

"I haven't heard," Helma said. "And no one called me."

"It's Binky," Roberta said. "Patrice is devastated."

"Poor Patrice," Eve added, shaking her yellow curls sorrowfully, her eyes genuinely brimming. "Binky was everything to Patrice."

"Will someone please tell me what happened?"

Helma asked, glancing from one sad face to the next, forgetting her tea bag and allowing it to steep longer than she liked.

"Binky's *dead*," Mrs. Carmon announced, folding her hands together over her stout waistline.

"Gone to poodle heaven," George Melville said. "There to sitteth at the right hand of Rin Tin-Tin."

"Rin Tin-Tin wasn't a poodle," Helma pointed out.

"He wasn't?" George asked in mock surprise.

Helma ignored him. "How did Binky die?"

"He had kidney problems," Mrs. Carmon told her. Mrs. Carmon owned a Pekingese and traded small-dog tips with Patrice. "Poor Patrice is so broken up."

"He was an old dog, I think," Eve said.

Mrs. Carmon nodded. "She always bought the 'senior pet' dog food for Binky."

"She phoned each of you to tell you?" Helma asked, remembering how her phone had gone unanswered while Walter David stood in her doorway.

"She didn't call me," George Melville said.

"You weren't home anyway," Roberta told him, immediately flushing, as if no one was aware of Roberta and George's relationship.

"I asked her to come over," Mrs. Carmon said, "but she didn't want to leave Binky alone."

"She called me, too," Eve added. "I didn't know what to say."

"You could have offered to bring her a pizza," George told her. Eve, the youngest librarian on the staff, lived with her boyfriend in an apartment above the Bellehaven Pizzeria.

"I didn't think of that. Pets get to be people, you know. I had a turtle once that died of that fungus stuff. I felt like I'd lost a human friend."

"So Patrice won't be working today?" Helma asked, finally rescuing her tea bag, wrapping the string twice around the bowl of the spoon to squeeze out the last of the liquid.

"Oh no. She's too grief stricken," Mrs. Carmon said.

Ms. Moon, the library director, entered the lounge. She raised her arms as if to embrace them all in a warm hug and smiled sorrowfully. "I see you've all heard of Patrice's loss. Roberta, if you'll take her shift on the reference desk today and Helma, if you'll finish Patrice's Baker and Taylor order; it needs to be faxed by four o'clock."

Ms. Moon paused, sighed dramatically, and closed her eyes for a long moment. All of life was consequential to Ms. May Apple Moon, significant with portent, ripe with meaning, and always worthy of comment.

Since becoming the director of Bellehaven Public Library two years ago, Ms. Moon, although still unaccountably tan, had exchanged her California slenderness for a more Northwest luxuriousness. She'd grown round and plush, expanding into her drapey, flowing clothes. Her laughter had deepened richly, her streaked hair thickened, and an unceasing flow of ideas sprouted in Bellehaven's moist climate.

"But our mission continues. There will be an informal harmony circle in fifteen minutes." Ms. Moon raised her arms again and returned to her office.

"Why do I always feel like she's about to hand me stone tablets from on high?" George asked, looking after Ms. Moon.

"Because you crave direction?" Roberta asked sweetly, touching a thin finger to George's arm.

Mrs. Carmon left the lounge, clucking her tongue. Helma followed after her and saw Mrs. Carmon drop a white sympathy-card-size envelope on Patrice's desk.

At her own desk, Helma retrieved a yellow pad and pencil for the meeting. Ms. Moon's staff meetings—her "harmony circles"—took place at the drop of a hat, disrupting well-laid daily schedules. "Communication is the cornerstone of every successful organization," Ms. Moon often said.

Roger Barnhard, the diminutive children's librarian, arrived from the downstairs children's library and joined the staff in the lounge, sitting between George and Eve. When Roberta told him of Binky's death, Roger replied sympathetically, "I have a new 'pet loss bibliography' in the children's department. Patrice might want to look at it."

Ms. Moon, juggling her bulletin board and notes, chose to squeeze a chair between Helma and Eve. Sometimes George Melville and Roger Barnhard made wagers where Ms. Moon would sit. She changed places at each meeting to "alter the group dynamic."

"Let us all join hands and be one with Patrice in her time of grief," Ms. Moon said, reaching for Helma's hand.

"No thank you," Helma said, folding her hands tightly together in her lap.

"Spouses, siblings, parents, yes," George Melville added, stroking his beard. "Dogs, cats, and canaries, no."

While her staff watched and waited, Ms. Moon briefly bowed her head, saying, "We are all—man and beast—interconnected on this earth."

Ms. Moon then got down to business and raised her flower-edged message board. On it, the t's crossed with curlicued flourishes, the i's dotted with round circles, were three items:

> Snow to Surf
> Card catalog disposal
> Overnight camp-outs

Helma tapped her fingers together. She hadn't had time to submit her camp-out memo. In fact, it was unprinted, still resting somewhere in the electronic oblivion of her computer.

"As you know," Ms. Moon began, "the Snow to Surf Race is seven weeks away."

The Snow to Surf Festival was Bellehaven's biggest annual event, corresponding to the Memorial Day holiday. The race itself was an eighty-five-mile relay race. It began at the ski area 4,500 feet up the mountain and wound its way over the hills and down the Nitcum

River, across Washington Bay to the shores of Bellehaven. Eighty-five miles of madness involving skiers, bicyclists, canoeists, and kayakers. Over two hundred
teams from all over the country and around the world
converged on Bellehaven each year to participate.

It had been another of Ms. Moon's ideas that the Bellehaven Public Library be represented by a team, "to pro-
mote reading and reinforce the library's integral position
in the community."

Happily, Helma Zukas didn't have any responsibility
in *that*. George Melville had appointed himself team
coach. Eve was competing in the downhill skiing leg and
Roger Barnhard, who'd vengefully taken up exhaustive
sports following his divorce, was the library's contender
in the mountain biking leg, although George Melville
said Roger was so small they might as well put him on
a Big Wheel.

Helma politely but disinterestedly listened as Ms.
Moon paused for a significantly long time before contin-
uing. "Curt and Stefan, our pages in training for the canoe leg of the race, have been forced to withdraw."

"Why?" Roberta asked.

"Their rock band has a gig," Eve supplied, then gig-
gled apologetically at Ms. Moon. "That's what I heard
anyway. In Seattle. It could be the Scalded Hog's big
break."

"And since the team must be composed of only library
employees in order to qualify for the local government
division, we either must find canoeists within the library
or cancel our team," Ms. Moon finished.

They were all silent, considering the unhappy likeli-
hood of losing their team. Roberta studied her thin
hands as Ms. Moon regarded them each meaningfully.
Helma gazed at the wall, mentally wording the new sign
she intended to place over the photocopy machines to
better explain the copyright law.

"I go sailing sometimes," Eve finally said. "I could
canoe, too."

"It's against the rules," Roger said.

"Skiing one leg of the race is library loyalty enough," George assured her.

"George will quiz the remaining staff," Ms. Moon said. She touched a beringed finger to *Card catalog disposal* on her board. "Now that our computer catalog has passed its six-month trial with flying colors we're ready to dispose of the old paper card catalog. The recyclers are coming to look at the cards tomorrow and then we'll be searching for a home for the cabinets."

"The passing of an era," George Melville said, holding his hand over his heart.

"It's about time," Eve said, wrinkling her nose.

"And for the next item," Ms. Moon clapped her hands together, her wide smile dimpling her tanned cheeks. "The library board has approved six Saturday-night camp-outs and the schools are thrilled, just thrilled. Our first overnight will be in two weeks, beginning with fourth-graders from Low Valley School." Ms. Moon held up the lid of a Gaylord book-pocket box. "In here are slips of paper bearing the date of each camp-out. Please choose one."

She held the orange box out to Helma, who never considered committing herself to the unknown. "I'd prefer an explanation," she told Ms. Moon. "What exactly are we drawing for?"

Ms. Moon regarded Helma in surprise, her mouth drawn into an O. "Why, to chaperone the camp-outs. Each librarian will take a turn, along with a classroom teacher or parent. It wouldn't be fair for Roger to chaperone *every* camp-out."

"Oh yes. Let's be fair," George said, holding out his hand for the box. "By all means."

"Chaperone?" Helma repeated.

"Only one night," Ms. Moon assured her. "That's all. Certainly a representative of the library should be present."

"Chaperoning hardly seems to be in the realm of professional librarianship," Helma protested.

"Oh, but it is," Ms. Moon replied enthusiastically.

"Think of how all those young people will view librarians after seeing us relaxed, playful, singing and sleeping with them around their imaginary campfires."

Helma waited for Roberta or Eve to protest but neither did. Suddenly she found herself wishing that Patrice, with whom she had the least congenial association in the library, was sitting at the table in her ramrod, pursed-lip stance of disapproval.

But no, they each took a slip of paper. Helma reluctantly plucked out the last slip in the bottom of the box.

May twenty-eighth.

"This is Memorial Day weekend," Helma pointed out, holding the May twenty-eighth slip.

"Oh, lucky you!" Ms. Moon cried. "That's the best one of all. It'll be part of a glorious celebration: the festival, the carnival and parade, the Snow to Surf Race."

"Those kids will be higher than kites," Roger Barnhard murmured beneath Ms. Moon's rapture. "Trust me. I know."

George Melville winked at Helma. "I warned you last night. But I know a way out. Trust me."

"How?" Helma inquired.

"Later."

"You didn't choose a date," Helma pointed out to Ms. Moon.

"If for some reason, any of you *can't* chaperone your allotted evening, I'll fill in for you." She laughed and playfully shook her finger at them. "Legitimate excuses only, of course. That's all for now. Our circle is adjourned."

"Go in peace," Helma unaccountably added in her head, believing Roger's warning of hyperactive children more than George's claim of knowing a way out, determined to somehow escape . . . *baby sitting*.

After the meeting, Helma entered Patrice's cubicle to find the Baker and Taylor book order. She gently set Patrice's blue geode paperweight next to a picture of Binky. The black poodle stood unnaturally upright on his hind legs, blue bows on his ears and a sparkling collar around his neck. Patrice's cubicle smelled faintly of lilac.

Helma sat at her own desk and perused Patrice's marked book catalog. Once titles were checked by the librarian, the catalog was passed on to Junie, who also doubled as George Melville's labeler. Junie typed up the orders and faxed or mailed them off to book jobbers and publishers.

Helma had just decided the unchecked *Economics of the American Revolution* was more pertinent to the library's collection than *On Your Marx, Go!*, when the busy workroom suddenly silenced. She raised her head from the catalog.

It was Patrice—red-eyed, face sagging with grief, her normally perfect champagne hair flat on one side and roughed up in the back. Tissues were scrunched and linted in her hand.

Patrice bowed her head, then unclasped her patent leather purse and removed a handful of square white envelopes. Wordlessly, she moved from desk to desk, gently laying an envelope in the center of each blotter. They all blatantly watched Patrice deposit her envelopes. Even George Melville stepped back and silently let her pass.

"Patrice, I'm . . ." Helma began as Patrice reached her desk.

Patrice raised her hand. "Not now. Please. But promise me you'll come." She gripped Helma's shoulder. "Please."

Helma winced at Patrice's grip and nodded so Patrice would release her.

"Thank you," Patrice whispered.

And just as quickly, her eyes averted and tight steps slightly askew, Patrice exited the library through the workroom door.

In her cubicle on the other side of Helma's, Eve picked up the square envelope and examined it. "What do you think it is?"

The envelopes were sealed. Helma slit hers with her

letter opener. "We could always look inside and find out," she told Eve.

"That's a good idea," Eve said, tearing off the end of her envelope.

It was an invitation—no, a request—to attend Binky's memorial service on Saturday morning.

"A funeral for a *dog*?" George Melville asked, holding out his black-edged note in two fingers, his arm extended.

"I think it's sweet," Eve told him.

"In her garden," Roberta added. "Have you ever seen her garden?"

"I've never been to Patrice's house," Helma told her.

"Has anybody?" George asked.

None of them had. Patrice was a thirty-year fixture in the Bellehaven Public Library, but aside from her passionate talk about Binky's antics and her exorbitant interest in the lives of the Bellehaven Public Library staff, Patrice rarely socialized with other library employees, to little regret.

"I read her garden will be on the Bellehaven Garden Tour this summer," Roberta said, "so it has to be pretty impressive."

"We should all go," George Melville said, his eyes sparkling. "I'll volunteer to be a pallbearer."

"Should we send flowers?" Eve asked.

"Or dog biscuit bouquets?" George countered.

"It's scheduled for eleven o'clock Saturday morning," Helma said. "Who's going to staff the reference desk?"

Ms. Moon joined them, holding her invitation. "I'll appear at the memorial briefly, out of respect, then return to tend the reference desk until your session at one, Roberta."

"But there will still be a period when the desk is unattended," Helma pointed out.

"Mrs. Carmon can cover for the simpler questions."

"Won't Mrs. Carmon be attending?" Helma asked. "She and Patrice are friends."

Ms. Moon shook her head. "Only the professional staff has been invited."

"I knew a professional library degree would win me perks someday," George Melville said.

A dog funeral. It was absurd but yes, Helma admitted she *was* curious about Patrice's home and garden. She'd attend for a short while anyway, maybe wear her black . . . no, she wasn't dressing in black for a dog. Her blue dress was perfectly adequate.

Just before her shift on the reference desk, George Melville leaned into Helma's cubicle. He held open a book to a picture of a canoe. "Reference question for you, Helma. Is this an all-wooden canoe?"

She glanced at it. "Of course not. It's wood and canvas. It looks like an Old Town."

George grunted and Helma looked into the satisfied grin on his face.

"Did you have one of these . . . Old Towns?" he asked.

"No. My uncle made me a cedar . . ." She stopped and studied George suspiciously. "This isn't idle curiosity, is it?"

"I knew you wouldn't toot your own horn, Helma. I suspected a Michigan girl like you knew canoes. What do you think of paddling in the canoe leg of the Snow to Surf Race in place of our budding rock stars?"

"I haven't been in a canoe in seventeen years."

"I bet you were good," George said.

Helma modestly ducked her head. "I was quite able."

"Well, think about this rare opportunity to participate in library sports history."

"No thank you. I couldn't possibly. It's out of the question."

George leaned farther into Helma's cubicle. Behind them, Roberta coughed and George leaned back. "You're forgetting one thing, Helma."

"What's that?"

"The date of the race."

"I haven't forgotten. It's Memorial Day weekend."

"And?"

Helma Zukas disliked guessing games. She closed her mouth, waiting for George to answer his own question.

"And," he continued. "If you were in the Snow to Surf Race you couldn't possibly be a chaperone for screaming prepubescent children camping out in the library on the Saturday night of Memorial Day weekend, could you?"

Having delivered that stunning bit of information, George swaggered back to his cataloging corner, leaving Helma deep in thought over the anguish of difficult choices.

At the reference desk, while Helma showed a disbelieving woman that the dictionary definition of "middle-aged" was indeed the years between forty and sixty, she heard her friend Ruth's unmistakable voice near the circulation desk.

"*I'd* call it a community event," Ruth was saying. "The whole community's definitely invited."

Ruth, wearing a multishaded purple dress she'd most likely constructed for herself, purple high heels, and carrying a lavender drawstring bag, towered over Mrs. Carmon. She held a poster showing herself in a slightly more risque but equally purple outfit. VIOLET VAMP, the poster advertising Ruth's upcoming show read. The name and the illustration were both taken from an obscure art journal called *Art Fringes*, which had published a feature on Ruth, catching her on the cresting edge of her Purple Phase, which Ruth likened to Picasso's Blue Period, or Bosch's golds.

Ruth and Mrs. Carmon scowled at each other, Ruth holding forth her poster, Mrs. Carmon refusing to take it. Helma coughed judiciously and Ruth turned and stalked toward Helma.

"This place is so provincial. Why can't you post this?"

"That bulletin board is designated for community-sponsored events," Helma explained. "Nonprofit organizations, public meetings, library events."

"So if I can get the boys at the fire department to sponsor me, I too can reside up there with blood drives and wetland hearings?"

"May I see your poster?" Helma asked, deflecting Ruth's question.

Ruth proudly held it out. "Do you like the way I enlarged *Violet Vamp*? Really catches your eye, doesn't it?"

Helma agreed. "But Ruth, I've never known an artist to charge admittance to a showing."

"Well, it's worth it. I'm going to wear that very same dress." Ruth leaned closer over the reference desk. Helma rescued the pencil holder before Ruth could knock it over. "Besides, I'm running a little low on cash."

"I heard there are several job openings in the courthouse."

"Hmmph," Ruth grunted, waving her hand in dismissal.

The last real job Ruth had held as far as Helma knew had been as a waitress during college, eighteen years ago. She'd been dismissed after dropping a hot roast beef sandwich in the lap of a man who'd pinched her. Ruth got by on her paintings, the kindness of friends, and something she vaguely referred to as "the insurance."

"So what's new in institutional life?" Ruth asked.

"Patrice's poodle died."

Ruth looked genuinely sad, dropping the poster to her side and twitching it against her leg. "Too bad. It's tough to lose an animal. I'd be sick if anything happened to my Max, wouldn't you?"

"Would I be sick if you lost your cat?"

"No, I mean yours: sweet Boy Cat Zukas."

"He's not my cat."

"Be honest. What would you do if the little dear suddenly vanished?"

"I'd have room on my balcony for flowers in place of cat dishes and a cat bed."

Ruth rolled her eyes. "Thank God you skipped

motherhood. Guess who I got a letter from today?"
Without pausing for Helma to guess, which she
wouldn't have, Ruth supplied, "Miss Higgins. Can you
believe somebody sent her a copy of the *Violet Vamp*
article from *Art Fringes*?" She tapped her poster for emphasis.

Miss Higgins had taught Latin in Scoop River, Michigan during Ruth and Helma's high school days, long
before Ruth and Helma had made their separate ways
to Bellehaven.

"What was her opinion?"

"She said she was amazed there were so many shades
of purple in the artist's palette."

Ruth tucked the poster beneath her arm. "I'd better go
find a willing wall for this thing. Gotta take advantage
of my fifteen minutes of fame."

Helma watched Ruth stride away from the desk, completely oblivious to the glances she drew.

"My library card number has to be changed," the
woman who'd been waiting behind Ruth loudly announced.

"Is there a problem with it?" Helma asked.

The woman thrust the card in front of Helma, her finger to the middle three numbers. "See? 666! These numbers are 666. I won't have the devil's numbers on my
library card."

Helma directed the woman to the circulation desk and
nodded to Eve, who'd just stopped by the reference
desk. In her arms she held an oversized, hardbound ret-
rospective of Flash Gordon comics. "George just told me
you might do the canoe in the Snow to Surf. That's really
cool."

"He suggested it," Helma told Eve, "but it's not a possibility."

Eve scratched her nose. "We've *got* to get somebody
from the library or we're out of the race. The team from
the city planning department would be pleased about
that, I'm sure. Roger's ex-wife's on it, you know."

"I didn't know," Helma said. She'd avoided listening

to tales of the children's librarian's divorce, but couldn't avoid the knowledge that it wasn't an amicable parting.

Eve nodded. "Wouldn't they love to beat the pants off each other?"

Curt, library page and budding rock star of Scalded Hog and ex–Snow to Surf canoeist, pushed a cart of books past the reference desk. Since he'd joined Scalded Hog, Curt had let his hair grow ponytail-long. A series of holes dotted his ears where, Eve told Helma, Curt hung gold rings. Curt had taken to keeping his face as expressionless as possible, a habit he let slip when he saw Eve.

"You guys playing this weekend?" Eve asked.

"At the Dirty Brew. You coming?"

"Wouldn't miss it."

Curt pointed to the Flash Gordon book. "That for the guy?"

Eve nodded. "My one and only. Volume two. He went through volume one in two days."

Curt nodded to Helma, expressionless again. "Good luck on the canoeing leg," and before Helma could protest, he was gone, ponytail bobbing, coolly pushing his cart of books toward the fiction stacks.

Between patrons, Helma read a chamber of commerce description of the Snow to Surf Race with its seven different legs: cross-country skiing, downhill skiing, running, biking, canoeing, mountain biking, sea kayaking. Eighty-five grueling miles. She'd never even attended the race. She *hadn't* canoed in seventeen years. True, she'd been more than an able canoeist, but it was ridiculous even to contemplate participating in a race as competitive as the Snow to Surf.

At that moment, one of the new computer card catalogs began bleating electronically as if it had been assaulted, drawing everyone's startled attention like a burglar alarm. A boy of about eleven stood in front of the screeching machine, grinning in delight.

The sight of him brought most sharply to Helma's mind the matter of the camp-out, the chaperonage of which Helma had drawn the same weekend as the Snow to Surf festivities. Twenty or thirty children in the library all night—sticky with cotton candy from the carnival, hyperactive from rides and the parade. All in the library, all night. With Helma. As she rose to rescue the computer, she stared at the smug smiling boy, picturing it.

"I just heard about your friend's purple art show," George Melville said when he came to relieve Helma on the reference desk.

"Did you talk to her?"

George shook his head. "Saw the poster in the men's restroom."

"*Labas, labas,*" Aunt Em said happily in Lithuanian when she heard Helma's voice. "Ah, Wilhelmina, how I look forward to Thursdays when you call."

Aunt Em pronounced Helma's name, "Vilhelmina," each syllable distinct and equally stressed.

"Do you have a cold, Aunt Em? Your voice sounds raspy."

"It's my old age. You're the first person I've talked to today besides Morris."

Morris was Aunt Em's cat, promoted in the past few years from barn to lap. Through her sliding glass doors, Helma saw scruffy Boy Cat Zukas stretched on her balcony railing, tail flicking, intently watching either Helma or his own reflection in the glass. Behind Boy Cat Zukas, clouds spread across the sky in layers of pearl and slate, obscuring both the sun and the most distant islands.

"Aunt Em, do you remember the canoe Uncle Tony built for me?"

There had been six brothers and sisters, including Helma's father, Uncle Tony and Uncle Mick, Aunt Aldona and Aunt Pansy. Now, cruelly, only Aunt Em, who'd been the oldest, remained, having watched all her siblings arrive on earth and depart.

"Ah, yes. My little *brolis*, Tony, God rest his soul. He built one for each of you on your twelfth birthday. He worked so hard that year because you and Mick's boy both turned twelve."

Aunt Em meant Helma's cousin Ricky, the scourge of Helma's youth. She was glad Aunt Em couldn't see her face. "Ricky managed to wreck his canoe the very first summer Uncle Tony gave it to him," Helma reminded Aunt Em.

She clenched her jaw as Aunt Em clucked sympathetically, just as everyone always had each of the innumerable times cousin Ricky got himself into trouble. "Poor Ricky had a hard life, with the way Mick died."

"Is my canoe still stored in your barn?"

"Up above the old broody pens. Stasys Boyaras—he still mows and fixes, even as old as he is—he takes it down and looks it over every spring."

"I didn't know that."

"Tony's canoes were *grazi* . . . beautiful, like an artist's. Stasys, he hopes you'll sell it to him someday."

"Then it's sound."

"If you wanted to, you could paddle it down Scoop River tomorrow. Are you coming home?" Aunt Em asked eagerly.

"Next fall, I think," Helma said.

"Ah, Wilhelmina. I'm getting older every day. Don't wait too long."

𝔰 chapter three 𝔰

PERIWINKLE

"**G**et over here!" Ruth's voice screeched in Helma's ear. "Hurry up!"

Helma stood beside her neatly made bed, barefoot, fresh from her shower, wrapped in a mint-green bath towel. Water dripped from her hair down the center of her back.

It wasn't a surprise that it was Ruth on the phone or that her voice palpitated with drama and emergency. What *was* startling was that it was only six-thirty in the morning. Since Ruth rarely got out of bed before ten o'clock it was likely Ruth had been up all night. A habit which Helma found unhealthy and completely dismaying.

"Ruth, you're screaming," Helma said calmly. Helma rose at six o'clock every morning in order to perform her complete morning ritual without having to rush. Being forced to rush unbalanced her entire day, as disorienting as oversleeping or the first day of Daylight Savings Time.

Ruth panted as if she couldn't catch her breath. "You would be, too. Get over here. I've ... He's ..."

Helma smoothed her bedspread and sat on the edge of her bed, reaching for a bottle of skin lotion and shaking it upside down. Time to buy a new bottle. "I'm

24

dressing for work, Ruth. I just stepped from the shower. If you had a difficult date last night, let's discuss it after I come home this evening."

A scrape of furniture sounded through the phone, then the indignant yowl of a cat, and finally a deep controlling gulp for air. "Helma Zukas," Ruth said in careful enunciation. "Are you familiar with the periwinkle that grows next to my garage on the alley?"

"Yes. Is it blooming?"

"At this moment, there's a man lying in it. And he's D-E-A-D."

Helma stood. The bottle of lotion slid to the floor, as did her mint-green towel. "Dead?" she repeated.

"I believe so. Now will you please come over?"

"I'm on my way."

Helma dropped the phone on the cradle and pulled on the underwear she'd set out to wear to the library. She left her dress hanging on the closet door. Not to view a body. Instead, she chose blue slacks and a two-year-old red sweater.

A man's body. Whose? Maybe Ruth was jumping to conclusions; *that* wouldn't be unusual. The man might be inebriated or unconscious in a faint. Helma's hair still dripped and clung to her head. She couldn't take the extra minutes to dry it. She rummaged through the hats on the top shelf of her closet and chose a billed sun hat, tucking her wet hair beneath it. She passed the mirror beside the door without a glance as she left her apartment.

Ruth's converted carriage house was on the "slope," a short drive away in the older, more genteel section of Bellehaven. The steep streets were empty except for a few early morning joggers.

Ruth stood waiting at the corner of her alley, dressed in paint-spattered jeans and a sweatshirt. Helma pulled her car to the curb, turned the wheels inward, set the brake, and got out. Ruth's eyes were bloodshot, her bushy hair impossible.

"Where is he?" Helma asked.

Ruth grabbed her arm. "Hurry up. What took you so long? Why didn't you drive in? Why park out here?"

"So I don't inadvertently destroy evidence."

They hurried down the alley side by side. A yellow dog whined through the fence of the Victorian house on the corner. Someone nearby practiced violin. A child, Helma guessed even in her hurry, recognizing the "tucka tucka ti ti" of the Suzuki method her nephew had played for her over the telephone. Ruth pulled her to a stop as they reached Ruth's sagging wooden garage.

"He's right there. See him?"

Ruth hung back and Helma cautiously approached the dense periwinkle.

First in view was the sole of a brown leather loafer, fairly new. Helma leaned forward. The man lay face-down. Beige, sharply creased polyester pants, slightly shiny, a blue baseball-style jacket pulled off his shoulders to reveal a silky green shirt, similar to the color of Helma's bath towel.

A purple periwinkle bud stood between the thumb and fingers of his left hand. The knuckles looked swollen and knotted, arthritic. A bald spot shone where his unusually blond hair had been combed across it, now disordered and standing out in greasy strands. Helma could see his high forehead but his face was hidden in the glossy foliage.

No, not inebriated or in a faint.

"When did you discover him?" Helma whispered.

"When do you think? Just before I called you. I was up all night, painting, and I went to the garage to get a shovel, you know, to trace around, and there he was. Lucky I didn't fall on top of him. Yuck."

Helma stepped to the side, examining the body from a longer view, noting the crushed periwinkle beside the body, as if he'd rolled or fallen before coming to his final rest.

In the past few years, Helma had had the misfortune to see other bodies, and each time, she was struck by their smallness, by the absence of being. Dead people never did look like they were "sleeping." She stood beside Ruth, gazing downward.

Ruth wrung her hands. "Should we drag him out of the bushes? Maybe he's not really dead."

Helma took in the stillness, the *weight* of the body, as if it were already sinking into the earth. "No. I'm certain he's dead. We can't touch him. I wonder what's taking the police so long."

"Oh," Ruth said, her eyes widening.

"You didn't call the police," Helma guessed.

"I called you."

"You'd better phone them now."

Ruth ran down the steps to her carriage house. Helma followed but when Ruth opened the door, she was assaulted by purple: violet, lavender, amethyst, heliotrope, lilac, mauve, plum, raspberry. Emanating from canvases hung around the walls of Ruth's kitchen, leaning against the counters, lying flat on the table. Even the air was tinged with violet.

Helma, who didn't own a single piece of purple clothing, never bought lavender notepaper, and avoided purple food, stepped back. "I'll stay with the body," she said, backing out the door.

The morning was silent, the sky featureless gray and the air slightly damp, rising up from Washington Bay. Through the firs and the big chestnut tree down the hill, she caught a glimpse of gray water.

The violin silenced and for a few moments there was no other sound but Helma's own breathing. No traffic or slamming doors. No dogs.

Helma Zukas bit her lip and glanced back toward Ruth's open door. She took another step closer to the body in the periwinkle, pausing only inches from it, light on her feet. Inhaling deeply, she bent down and pulled the vines away from the dead man's face. Only one side was visible and it was darkly mottled.

As she suspected, he wasn't young. In fact, Helma guessed he was in his sixties. He had a greasy look to him, a moustache as waxy as his hair, which Helma sur-

mised was dyed that bright yellow. He looked like the
type of man who'd neglected his teeth early in life.

There might be nothing sinister here. A heart attack
victim, struck down while strolling the alley on his daily
constitutional, stumbling and falling tragically into the
periwinkle. A wife might be frantically phoning the
neighbors and searching the alleys for him at that very
instant.

But then Helma spotted the marks around the man's
neck. A thin brownish stripe highlighted by three evenly
spaced indentations, then nothing, then another round
indentation. She pushed the leaves aside, trying to get a
better view.

"Helma! What are you doing?"

She let loose of the periwinkle and straightened. "Just
looking. Are the police on the way?"

"Is that a rhetorical question? Of course they're on
their way. They can hardly wait to get here."

Sirens, at least three of them, approached, howling.
Two dogs from up the street joined in.

Within moments the alley was blocked by police cars,
lights gyrating, radios buzzing. Neighbors emerged,
some still in nightclothes, to watch from the other side
of the police cars. Two young boys hung eagerly over
the fence across the alley.

Helma and Ruth retreated to Ruth's rough lawn beneath the willow tree, admiring the orchestrated movements of the police. Up went the yellow crime tape.
Picture and note taking, inspection, no wasted movements. And all the time, their efficiency was heightened by a brightness in the eyes, a murmur of excitement, and . . . eagerness.

"The chief's on his way," one of the policemen said.

Ruth elbowed Helma and raised her eyebrows. "Chief
Knight-in-Shining-Armor," she whispered. "Bet you
wish you'd combed your hair."

Despite the situation, Helma touched the cap that covered her wet hair. She fingered the ribbing of her old

sweater. "Murder is hardly the time to be concerned with fashion," she told Ruth.

"There's *no* inappropriate time," Ruth answered.

"Which of you found him?" asked a young policeman Helma recognized as Officer Sidney Lehman.

"Hi, Sid," Ruth said. "I did. This morning about six. Then I phoned my friend Helma, here."

"Before the police?"

Ruth shrugged, stretching herself taller until she was able to peer down at Officer Lehman from the bottom of her eyes. "Yeah. So?"

Chief Wayne Gallant, tall, his hair in becoming disarray and dressed in a black jogging suit, joined them. Helma hadn't seen his car arrive and she was caught unawares, recovering herself just as she was about to pull the bill of her cap lower to obscure her face.

"Miss Zukas, Miss Winthrop," he said formally, glancing at Officer Lehman's notes and then conferring with him in tones too low for Helma to hear, despite taking the opportunity to slide a step closer to the two men.

Chief Gallant joined the men around the body, examining the immediate area. The dead man still lay as Ruth had found him, on his stomach, his face obscured by vines.

"Hey, lady. Did you kill that guy?" one of the boys hanging over the fence called to Ruth.

"It's getting late," Helma told the boys, glancing at her wrist before she realized she hadn't taken the time to don her watch. "Have you brushed your teeth for school yet?"

"Nah. We got plenty of time."

"We never have as much time as we think we do," she replied in her silver-dime voice. "Now go inside and prepare yourselves for school."

"Geez." But the two heads disappeared.

Ruth appraised the policemen. "I can see a couple here I wouldn't mind surrendering myself to."

Ruth laughed her too-loud laugh, not noticing the plump man in plainclothes who glanced at her speculatively, then jotted in his notebook. He had unusually small hands and small feet, a portly body and a short neck, reminding Helma of a toy figure children knocked down and which continually swayed upright again. Round glasses widened his eyes. A small moustache that might have aged his pink-cheeked face was negated by his military-style haircut and the smooth skin that bulged at his collar.

Chief Gallant rejoined Ruth and Helma. "Do either of you know who this man is?"

"It's hard to recognize a guy lying on his face," Ruth replied. "Most guys, anyway."

"That's true," Helma agreed.

"Did you hear any noises last night?" the chief asked Ruth.

Ruth shook her head. "I was painting and I had the radio on. Loud."

"You were home all evening?"

Ruth shook her head. "From about ten-thirty or eleven on. I went out for a while."

Chief Gallant turned to Helma. "And when did you first learn of the body?"

"When Ruth phoned me at six-thirty. I came over immediately and viewed the scene. The victim appears to be an elderly man, I believe in his mid-sixties despite the blond hair. I noticed the unusual marks on his neck. I presume that indicates foul play. Do you suspect he was strangled?"

Chief Gallant grinned at Helma and scratched his head with the eraser end of his pencil. The skin crinkled at the outer edges of his eyes. "Helma . . . Miss Zukas, your powers of observation have gained my respect in the past few years. I'm interested in hearing any of your thoughts regarding this death."

"As I am yours," Helma told him.

"Now Miss Winthrop, do you believe the body may have been present when you arrived home last night," he glanced at his notebook, "about ten-thirty or eleven?"

"I don't think so. I walked up the alley from Johnson

Street so the streetlight would have been shining on him."

"You walked?"

The man Helma suspected was a plainclothes detective stood a little to the right, behind Chief Gallant, watching Ruth, avidly listening, pen poised over notebook.

"Mm-hmm. I went out for a drink. To Joker's. Being a law-abiding citizen I never drink and drive. But then, I usually don't walk, either."

"But last night no one gave you a ride?"

"They might have, but a creep was bugging me so I left."

"In what way was he bothering you?"

"You know. A short guy who fantasizes climbing a tall woman. Then turns on her if she doesn't think he's the cutest little banty rooster that cocked the walk."

"I see."

Finally, after more photos and measurements and items slipped in plastic bags, the dead man's body was ready to be removed. Helma and Ruth remained beside Ruth's sidewalk, watching. The body was turned over and Chief Gallant motioned to them. "If you're up to it, you can tell me if either of you recognize him."

Both Ruth and Helma stepped forward. Helma tried to concentrate only on his features, not the marks from the periwinkle or the settling of blood. His shirt collar had been pulled up to cover the impressions on his throat, marks Helma Zukas was very interested in examining. He had a large nose, a face that tapered sharply to his chin, and beneath the mottled red he was tan: a dark, spotty, artificial tan that browned his wrinkled face like an antiquing kit. She was right: mid-sixties but she'd guess making efforts to appear younger. Small, she doubted he was much taller than she was.

"He's not at all familiar to me," Helma said.

Ruth looked down at the body, frowning. "Me neither."

"What was his name?" Helma asked the chief. "Surely you found identification on his body."

"We have to verify it first," he told her. "I appreciate your assistance." He slipped his notebook in the pocket of his jogging pants as the body was taken away, relaxing as if a switch had turned off his official capacity. "Interesting that we have a death in Bellehaven and you two are involved."

He didn't add the word "again," but Helma heard it there, hovering at the end of his sentence.

"I'd hardly use the term 'involved,' " Helma told him.

"There must be a mysterious magnetic force at work here," he said. "Oh." He motioned to the plainclothes man with the small feet and hands. "This is Detective Carter Houston. Just joined our ranks two weeks ago."

Detective Carter Houston didn't offer his hand. He nodded briskly without smiling, his movements brief and precise. He had to look up into Ruth's face.

"Just got your detective badge, did you?" Ruth asked.

The detective blushed. "I've had extensive experience and training."

"Well, congratulations," Ruth said. "We're all grateful to hear *that*."

Ruth was engaging in what she called "teasing," but Detective Carter Houston stiffened, his lips tight, his dapper little feet tidily side by side.

"Your cap is becoming, Helma," Chief Gallant said. "Stylish."

Now it was Helma's turn to flush under Ruth's teasing gaze.

"Thank you," she said. "If we're finished here, I must leave now. It's Friday and I have to prepare for work."

At first, as Helma reshowered and dressed for the library, the mottled face of the dead man in the periwinkle kept intruding, causing her to pause in her toilet, momentarily too stunned to continue. Who was he? What had taken place in the alley beside Ruth's garage? And those marks on his neck?

But then she faced herself squarely in her bathroom mirror. "*Do not think about it,*" she said aloud, so stern she convinced even herself.

So when she entered the library workroom two hours and fifty-six minutes late and Ms. Moon rushed forward, her lips pursed and making little "poot poot poot" sounds, at first Helma was bewildered.

"How were you informed so quickly?" Helma asked.

"Jack's been here since five and he told us."

Jack, the library janitor, had a sister-in-law in the police department, a police band radio in his house, and an extensive collection of police procedural mysteries— all belonging to the library and few of them properly checked out—in the oversized room called the "janitor's closet."

"He said the address belonged to a friend of yours," Ms. Moon said. "Do you know the cause of death?"

"The location was purely coincidental. Since he was an elderly man, it may have been a heart attack." Helma crossed her fingers behind her back, seeing again the marks around the man's neck.

"This cycle of his eternal route was complete," Ms. Moon went on. "Life begins anew, ever more joyous, ever more knowledgeable." She fingered her crystal earrings, dropped her voice and hesitantly asked. "Were you in time to see anything unusual? Perhaps a miasma hovering above his body?"

"I'm afraid not. Excuse me," Helma said, edging around Ms. Moon toward her desk.

Patrice's cubicle was empty, her desk lamp off. A red-foil pot of petunias sat in the middle of Patrice's blotter. If only Helma hadn't promised Patrice she'd attend Binky's memorial service tomorrow.

Eve leaned across the shelves separating their cubicles. "Geez, Helma. I heard somebody got murdered and you were there."

"Only by chance," Helma told her.

"Was it gross?"

"Tut, tut, child," George Melville interrupted, carrying

a cup of coffee from the lounge. "Don't be gruesome." He turned to Helma. "Was it?"

"It was simply an accidental death. I hardly saw anything."

George Melville raised his eyebrows. "We'll see," he said.

"Did you read Kara Cherry's column in the *Daily News* last night?" Eve asked.

"I didn't get to the feature section," Helma told her.

"She found out we're getting rid of the card catalog and wants it saved for posterity."

"Why?"

"For future socioanthropological research," George said. "Her best argument was that if you studied the cards that were dirtiest from patrons thumbing through them, you'd know which subjects most interested the mid- to late-twentieth-century populace."

"Or what subject teachers were assigning," Helma offered.

"Or that people interested in certain subjects don't wash their hands," Eve said.

George gave Eve a look of admiration. "That's commendable deductive reasoning, Eve."

"But there are six banks of card catalogs and over half a million cards," Helma said. "We don't have room to store them."

"The indefatigable Ms. Cherry called for the museum to take up our fallen standard," George said.

"Maybe there's a place, you know, like in *Raiders of the Lost Ark,* where you can put stuff like that," Eve said.

"And never find it again."

"At least it would be saved," Eve said.

"You sound like my first wife."

Both Helma and Eve looked to George for further enlightenment. He'd come late in life to librarianship and rather by accident or design, rarely divulged details of his personal life. Helma wasn't even certain of George Melville's origin, only that it wasn't Washington state.

Sometimes she thought she detected a touch of an upper-west accent: Montana or Wyoming.

"Well, back to implementing the never-ending flow of knowledge to the public," George said and left them gazing after him.

"Do you think 'first wife' means 'first and only' or 'first of several'?" Eve asked.

Instead of joining Eve in her pondering, Helma asked. "Did Ms. Moon reassign Patrice's reference desk hours?"

Eve raised her hand. "All mine. Lucky me. Oh. I'm so glad you're doing the canoe leg of the Snow to Surf Race."

"I didn't . . ."

"Thanks. Really. It would be a drag to have to back out now after all the training and hype and stuff."

Helma sat down at her desk. She slipped an M&M beneath her tongue. When Helma was little her father had told her proudly that M&M's were developed for World War II soldiers to carry: melt in your mouth, not in your pack. She felt a tug of a tribute toward history each time she sucked one to its chocolatey center. Plain M&M's. Helma had never tried a peanut M&M.

The Snow to Surf Race. Canoes. Her own canoe, that beautiful, sleek cedar canoe she'd paddled on Scoop River so many years ago, with its caned seats and ash thwarts. Mostly paddling by herself; it was a canoe that responded well to one person, light as a leaf on water. Uncle Tony had built Helma's canoe with her size in mind: lighter than Ricky's, smaller, intended for a person who preferred solo paddling. "It's a good fit," Uncle Tony had said proudly the first time he saw Helma effortlessly execute a pivot turn past an old sunken tangle of logs left from lumbering days on Scoop River.

For a few years when Helma was little, Uncle Tony had left Michigan to live alone in Maine—Helma's mother had claimed it was after Uncle Tony had a violent quarrel with Aunt Sophie over an uprooted forsythia bush. He'd timbered in the Maine woods, spending his winter months learning to build cedar strip canoes, and when he'd returned, it was to present Aunt Sophie with a canoe so exquisitely beautiful it now hung from the ceiling rafters over the Jesuit missionary display in the Scoop River Museum.

The canoe Uncle Tony had made for Helma was hers, her own personal canoe, built for Helma Zukas and no one else.

It was twelve-thirty in Michigan. Helma's brother Bruce was most likely working in the studio behind his house.

As a child Bruce had "whittled," making rubberband guns and wooden soldiers to shoot, duck decoys and monsters, caricatures so real they could make his victims cry. His whittling had progressed to fine carving and now he worked with the delighted passion of a man who discovers he can make all the money he needs doing what he loves to do most.

Bruce answered on the first ring, sounding distracted, deep in his work. "Billie. This is an unusual time for you to call."

"I wish you wouldn't call me that."

"Sorry. You caught me with my guard down. What's up?"

"I'd like you to ship my canoe to Washington."

"The canoe Uncle Tony made? In Aunt Em's barn? What for?"

"I may participate in a local race."

Bruce laughed. "No lie? Sure. I can do that. I'll call a freight company tomorrow and let you know their rates."

"It's more pressing than that. If I decide to participate I need to begin training at once. I'd like it shipped by air freight as soon as possible. By Monday if you can."

Bruce whistled into the phone. "It'd be cheaper to buy a new canoe, Bil . . . Helma. Flying it out to Washington will cost a fortune."

"No. I'd feel far more confident if I were able to paddle my own canoe," Helma assured Bruce.

❧ chapter four ❦

SATURDAY MEMORIAL

Helma's mother Lillian called on Saturday morning from the retirement apartments across town.

"Helma, dear. I have the newspaper right here in front of me. Isn't this address where they found the dead man near Ruth's house?"

Lillian had moved from Michigan to Bellehaven after Helma's father died five years ago. She'd been a content widow, but following a brief fling at dating several months ago, Lillian had suddenly traded her four-door sedan for a low-slung red compact, added two exercise classes and a hiking club to her numerous club commitments, and only two weeks ago Helma had caught sight of her mother exiting the Gap, face rosy, a bulging package under her arm.

Helma leaned across the counter and popped the slice of white bread out of her toaster to wait until after the phone call. Her copy of the *Bellehaven Daily News* hadn't made it to the paper holder that morning.

"It's in Ruth's vicinity," Helma told her mother. "Does the paper name the victim?"

"Mmm. Let's see. 'Joshman Lotz, sixty-six.' That's all. 'Police are still investigating.' They're always investigating, aren't they? Digging up things? Do you ever see Chief Gallant, Wilhelmina?" she asked hopefully.

37

"Only in passing."

"Oh. Brucie called last night. He said he's shipping that old canoe all the way out here for you for a *race*?"

"I might participate in the canoe leg of the Snow to Surf Race, on the library's team. I haven't decided yet."

"Do you think that's wise, Helma?"

"What do you mean, Mother?"

"Your Uncle Tony built that canoe such a long time ago. It's old, and you . . . well, you *are* almost thirty-nine."

"I exercise or walk every day. I know I'll need to train, but I'm in very good shape." Without thinking, Helma flexed her shoulders, as if they already ached after a day's paddling.

"When I was your age," Lillian said. "All three of you children were in high school, nearly grown up. Why, at your age, I could have almost been a grandmother. I was ready for it back then. My life was settled."

"I know, Mother," Helma said.

It was sunny and surprisingly warm for an April morning when Helma opened her balcony door and threw her blue slipper—the first thing that came to hand—at Boy Cat Zukas. He was crouched on her railing, hacking in loud barks, the scraggly sides of his lean body spasming, neck extended and his mouth stretched wide.

"Oh, Faulkner," she said as her slipper sailed over the railing and down three stories to the rocky slope of the bay.

Boy Cat Zukas paused in his hacking long enough to leap up to her roof where, above her head, he continued his efforts to eject stomach contents. Helma closed and locked her balcony door, pulled her opaque shades, and fled her apartment.

She pulled her car next to the curb behind Eve's orange Volkswagen. Ms. Moon's baby-blue Volvo sat in Patrice's driveway. It was five minutes to eleven.

Patrice lived on the north end of Bellehaven, in a

house that had been in her family, she said once, "since statehood." Helma got out, bearing a tray of bakery cookies, and walked slowly up the walk, trying to take in Patrice's spring garden. Her small, cottagelike house nestled among luxuriant shrubbery winding and twining and bending over stone walls. Candytuft cascaded, ivy climbed amongst brilliant banks of azaleas, roses unfolded coppery new leaves. Two robins splashed in a birdbath while another pecked in the dark soil of a freshly turned garden space. A goldfinch swooped past.

And it was only April. Sometimes in April, snowstorms blasted from Lake Michigan into Scoop River, whitening a still-dead and thawing land where crocuses were timidly just raising their purple and orange heads.

"Around back," Eve said, emerging from a grape arbor at the side of the house, dressed in a flowered shirt that nudged the knees of her jeans. "Is this delicious or what? Wait'll you see the backyard. Now we know what Patrice does when she's not at the library."

"It must take all her free time."

"I'll say. Unless she pays a fleet of lawn drones."

The back garden was even more dazzling. A feast. A green and colorful world all its own, accented and punctuated by more natural stone walls, a stone patio, trellises, and arbors. Helma remembered a book she'd loved which Aunt Em had given her as a child: *The Secret Garden*.

"Hi, Helma," Roberta said dreamily, her body shockingly narrow in a calf-length blue dress with red vertical stripes. "Isn't this fabulous? I think I've died and gone to heaven." Then she covered her mouth and glanced at Patrice, who stood beside a white wicker table that held punch and artfully arranged crustless sandwiches and bite-size pastel cakes.

Patrice had shrunk since Wednesday, her skin a finer, papery grain, her eyes lowered in mourning. Helma felt a dark twinge of guilt for never once having asked—or even cared—about Binky's health during all the years she'd known Patrice.

"Look at this," Roberta continued, tapping her toe on the stone patio. Embedded between the cool, flat stones were polished stones: agates, obsidian, and quartz, shining like jewels. "Patrice said she polished them herself in a rock tumbler. Who would have believed *that*?"

"People always surprise you," Helma said, "if you allow them to."

Patrice came forward and took Helma's tray. "I think we're all here now," she said, nodding toward Roger Barnhard, who was just entering her garden, dressed in tight, shiny black bicycling clothes and carrying a black bike helmet. Helma was frankly surprised. She'd certainly never considered the children's librarian a *muscular* man before today. Eve's eyes met Helma's, an eyebrow raised in a startled look of appreciation.

George Melville caught their exchange and glanced over at Roger. "Rog could pose as a divorce lawyer's poster boy," he commented.

"Your gardens are exquisite, Patrice," Helma said. "Did you design them?"

Patrice nodded. "Designed and built. All of them."

George Melville bit into a cookie. "You must have found an Irish dike builder for the stone walls and patios."

"I built them myself," Patrice said firmly, as if she'd caught George not paying attention.

George's eyes widened and Helma caught a glimpse of something new in his regard of Patrice.

"Everyone needs an activity to keep them busy," Patrice said with a hint of the old self-importance to which they were accustomed. "Preferably one that also beautifies the world."

Ms. Moon fluttered forth from a towering display of rhododendrons. Glowing, smiling, her honey-blonde hair becomingly tousled about her round face. She sighed and touched Patrice's arm. "I'd like to give a segment of the eulogy, Patrice, to give meaning to your loss, to say a few words about the grief and joy of rebirth."

Patrice straightened the luncheon napkins. "Neither

Binky nor I believed in rebirth, Ms. Moon. Once around is enough."

Ms. Moon, although rebuffed, continued to smile, swaying a little as if she heard distant music.

Binky's grave lay beneath a weeping birch newly leafed out in the corner of the garden. "I hope weeping birches aren't like weeping willows," George Melville said to Roger in an undertone. "Their roots get into everything."

They gathered around the tiny grave that was spread with a professionally woven blanket of bright spring flowers. A granite tombstone, engraved with: "Binky. 16 years old. Valiant Friend," stood at its head, a silver-framed photograph of Binky the poodle chewing mischievously on a high heel shoe propped against it.

"I'd like to read a passage from Binky's favorite book, *The Poodle Cousin*," Patrice began. "Terry Berry sat like a princess in her pink room, freshly fluffed and curled and white . . ."

Helma's palms began to perspire. The mongrel dogs from her childhood, who'd followed them to school and wandered the neighborhood and frequently died on the road—loved lavishly but never allowed indoors, fed the least expensive food—had been laid to rest by the fence line in childishly marked graves, markers that were inevitably faded away or gone after the next winter's thaw.

She couldn't listen to Patrice's raspy, emotional voice. She looked away when Eve patted Patrice's arm and Patrice, instead of flinching, leaned toward Eve. Helma closed her eyes and pretended she was somewhere else, away from this strange, sad ceremony in this beautiful garden. She imagined sitting by the bay with the waves lapping on shore, scouring the graveled beach clean.

But then, the image of the dead man in Ruth's periwinkle invaded her reverie and Helma was unwillingly thrust into the present, hearing the unbearably tragic voice of Patrice finish the memorial with, "Farewell, dear friend."

Tears slid down Eve's cheeks. Ms. Moon stood with

her hands over her heart. Roberta stared down at her feet. George and Roger Barnhard exchanged inscrutable glances.

Patrice closed *The Poodle Cousin*, wiped away a tear, and said, "I'm really not prepared to have people inside my house but you're welcome to enjoy my gardens and have a bite to eat before you leave."

They moved uncertainly toward the tableau of food and wicker furniture, glancing at one another, trying to decipher Patrice's mixed messages.

On her way home from Binky's memorial service, Helma stopped by the 7-Eleven and bought a replacement copy of the *Bellehaven Daily News*.

"How about a lottery ticket with that?" the clerk asked her. "It's up to seven million smackers."

"About the same as the odds," Helma said, holding out her hand for her change.

She sat behind the steering wheel in the 7-Eleven parking lot and read the brief article in the lower corner of the front page. BODY DISCOVERED IN ALLEY. Joshman Lotz, sixty-six, just like her mother had said. Helma knew Sunspot Acres, Joshman Lotz's address: a ramshackle group of cabins and apartments at the southern edge of Bellehaven, a reputed hippie haven during the sixties and now an address notorious at the library for overdue and irretrievable library materials.

The article said the cause of death was as yet unknown. It didn't mention foul play or Joshman Lotz's history. She turned to the obituaries but it was too soon for an announcement there. Helma refolded the newspaper and set it on the passenger seat.

Her interest was only based on curiosity. This murder had nothing to do with her; it wasn't about to interrupt her personal and professional life, as other unfortunate incidents had in the past.

Helma was reaching for her ignition key when someone tapped on her window. A middle-aged man stood there, balding, wearing glasses. He smiled and made rolling-down-the-window motions. Helma glanced to be sure there were plenty of witnesses in the 7-Eleven parking lot before she did.

"Yes?"

"I was admiring your car," he said, gazing past her at the dashboard, the upholstery. "I had one almost identical."

"Thank you."

"All original?"

"I beg your pardon?"

He sighed. "Unless I'm mistaken, this is the original paint job. It looks like all the original accessories, too."

"Of course. Why would I change them?"

"Are you the original owner, too?"

As a rule, Helma Zukas didn't provide personal information to strangers but she was also a perceptive judge of people and it was apparent this man meant no harm.

"It was my high school graduation gift, twenty-one years ago."

"She's a beauty." He sighed again and shook his head, his eyes soft. "Here's my card. If you ever want to sell her, I'd like to make an offer."

Helma took his card, noting that Tobias Stockman was an accountant. He stood on the sidewalk in front of the 7-Eleven, watching wistfully as she pulled out of the parking lot. Helma hadn't thought of her Buick as being of female gender before and found it curious that Tobias Stockman had decided so after such a brief association.

She drove home through downtown Bellehaven. Since the mall had opened two months ago, traffic flowed more freely through the now quieter city core. Parking was easier, too. In fact, it was rare not to find a vacant space right on the main street. She stopped for a red light and noted the GOING OUT OF BUSINESS SALE! banner across the front window of Catherine's Fine Dresses.

On the doormat in front of Helma's apartment lay a newspaper-wrapped object, tied with a piece of brown twine knotted into a bow. Helma warily picked it up and felt its weight: light. She pulled one end of the string. The newspaper unfolded to reveal the blue slipper she'd thrown at Boy Cat Zukas. There was no note, no explanation, only her slipper in newspaper. She swallowed and looked behind her and down into the parking lot.

The door of 3E opened and Mrs. Whitney emerged, a single curler still twisted in her white hair. She pointed a cane at the slipper. "Walter David left that for you. Wasn't that sweet?"

"I was wondering. How did he know it was mine?"

"I happened to be sweeping the landing when he brought it. He said he was working below the building and it nearly hit him on the head." She looked curiously at the slipper, then at Helma.

Helma rewrapped her slipper. It was going in the washing machine immediately. "It was an accident," Helma explained. "I've never seen you use a cane, Mrs. Whitney," she said, changing the subject.

"Ah, my arthritis is giving me fits today." She smiled her shining smile. "No sympathy please. But here, I want to show you the latest pictures of the great-grandchildren."

Mrs. Whitney pulled four photographs from her dress pocket. Helma knew there were three great-grandchildren under the age of four, but she was unable to tell them apart. "They've grown," she said, hoping she wasn't looking at four photos of the same child.

"Haven't they? Meg may come up this summer."

Mrs. Whitney's daughters had moved to California years ago. "Bellehaven is my home," Mrs. Whitney had told Helma. "I couldn't go to that hot place with all those surfers and fancy movie people."

"Did you know the man they found dead yesterday?" Helma asked, handing back the photos of the similar round-faced children. "Joshman Lotz? The paper said he was a Bellehaven native."

"I knew the family," Mrs. Whitney told her, shaking her head the way people did over lost causes. "This used to be a small town. Everybody knew everybody. He was younger than me but he was a wild one. He wasn't too old to be up to no good when he died. There are a lot of nice houses and expensive things on the Slope. Why else would he be up there but to cause trouble?"

Helma hadn't thought of that. It *was* a long way— further than just distance—from Sunspot Acres to the Slope.

"One of his brothers broke away," Mrs. Whitney went on. "He changed his name and became a podiatrist. He's still in town—Dr. Robertson. There's not much we can do about the family we're born into, is there? Although if it had been *me,* I'd have changed my name *and* left town, too."

"I imagine there will be more details in a few days," Helma told Mrs. Whitney. "I meant to tell you, *Porcelain Baby Dolls of the 19th Century* is still checked out but I put a hold on it for you."

"Thank you, dear. You make me feel like I have my very own librarian."

Helma carried her slipper inside and bolted the door behind her. She removed a container of leftover shrimp and pasta salad from her refrigerator, burped open the Tupperware seal and set it on the counter to reach room temperature. Helma Zukas disliked overly hot or overly cold foods.

While the salad warmed, she critically eyed the cover of her newest Smithsonian magazine, focusing on the clouded background of a pastoral Midwest scene, reaching for her scissors.

Helma did not knit or crochet, having tried as a girl but losing patience with the process once she equated it with the guessing games she disliked so much. One never really knew if what was worked on so diligently would be wearable, or even flattering if it did fit.

But since she was a child, Helma had found secret delight in Cutting Out Things, soothed by the experience of edging around a zebra's flicking tail or the cowlick of a turned head, cutting so closely not a speck of background showed and not a stray hair was lost.

For years she'd cut out figures and clouds and trees and towering buildings, tidily disposing of both the paper shreds and the cut objects themselves once she was finished, satisfied by the activity, indifferent to the results.

Quite by accident, mainly due to the orderliness of Miss Zukas's mind, she began cutting out things by theme: by hues of color or similarity of shape or species of animal or object. From there, it was logical to group her cuttings together, then to store them in neatly labeled file folders and finally to glue them onto posterboard in arrangements that sometimes pleased her and frankly sometimes shocked her.

Each arrangement she completed unaccountably embarrassed Helma and after keeping it in her bedroom for a few days she folded it in half and put it in her garbage, never showing anyone.

Helma was cutting around the misty edge of her second cumulus cloud from the Smithsonian cover, her pasta salad almost to room temperature, when her doorbell rang. She started, then swept the paper scraps into her hand, dropped them in her trash, put away her scissors, and tucked the cumulus cloud beneath her *TV Guide* before she answered the door, mentally bracing herself in case it was Walter David coming to explain his retrieval of her blue slipper.

But it wasn't Walter David. She blinked, trying to place the well-dressed, rotund man who stood before her.

"Miss Zukas," he said, not smiling, businesslike. "I'm Detective Carter Houston. I'd like to ask you a few questions."

She glanced at his hands and feet, remembering the detective in Ruth's alley, the body. She stood in her partially open door, aware of an unfounded but instantaneous and full-blown dislike for Detective Carter Houston. It happened sometimes.

"Pertaining to what matter?"

"The death of Joshman Lotz."

"And who might he be?" Helma politely inquired.

His eyes tightened, but only slightly. "The man found dead behind Ruth Winthrop's house."

"You mean in the alley, don't you? You see, her house is the former carriage house so its front actually faces the alley. Technically, the body was found in *front* of Ruth Winthrop's house."

"You know what I mean," he said peevishly.

"I would think the police would always strive to be technically correct."

"May I come in?"

Helma glanced meaningfully at the detective's feet and opened her door. He wiped the sole of each shiny black shoe once and entered, flagrantly staring at her apartment's interior. Helma motioned him to the rocking chair that blocked his view of as much of her apartment as possible, pretending not to watch how he tried to keep the rocking chair upright and steady as he sat. She sat opposite him and folded her hands in her lap. Out came his notebook, identical to Chief Gallant's.

"I'd like to confirm the sequence of events yesterday," he said. Beneath Detective Houston's precise speech, Helma detected a drawl, under control but definitely present. "Miss Winthrop phoned you at six-thirty in the morning to tell you there was a dead man in the ivy?"

"Periwinkle," Helma corrected.

"And you drove to her house immediately. Am I correct?"

"So far."

The detective stared at Helma, rarely blinking, his gaze boring into her. He touched one end of his moustache as if he were about to twirl it. "Would you say your friend was upset?"

"Yes, I'd say my friend was upset."

"But she didn't recognize the deceased?"

"You were present when she stated she didn't."

"Mm-hmm," he said, making a mark in his notebook without taking his eyes off Helma. "Do you know where Miss Winthrop was on Thursday night?"

"In her house, painting."

"Prior to that?"

"No, I don't."

"I believe your cat wants in." He nodded his head toward her balcony door, where Boy Cat Zukas was stretched upward to his full length, belly pressed against the glass, pawing at the door.

"He's not my cat," Helma said.

"I see. I've been led to understand your friend lives a slightly unsettled life."

"Ruth Winthrop is an artist."

"Meaning?"

"Meaning nothing. It's simply a fact. I'm uncertain what your interpretation of 'unsettled' is, or how it pertains to the death of a man from Sunspot Acres."

Detective Houston's eyes definitely *did* narrow this time. "How did you know Lotz was from Sunspot?"

"It was in this morning's *Bellehaven Daily News*," Helma told him, meeting his gaze squarely.

He nodded knowingly, almost smugly, and Helma rose, wanting him out of her apartment at once. "If you have questions concerning Ruth's whereabouts or activities, please speak with her. I'm sure she can answer with more authority than I can."

"Have you spoken to her this morning?" he asked, rising, putting his notebook away, touching one finger to the top of Helma's bookcase as if he might check for dust.

"No, I haven't."

"Where were you this morning?"

"At a graveside memorial service." She edged the detective toward her door.

"Which cemetery?"

"It was in a private garden. Now if you'll excuse me, I have work to do."

"We'll be speaking again soon," he said at her door.

"I seriously doubt it."

Once her door was closed and locked and the deadbolt

secured, Helma hurried to her phone and dialed Ruth's number.

It rang eight times and Helma hung up. She slid open her balcony door and stood looking out over the shimmering waters of Washington Bay, folding and refolding her carefully excised cumulus cloud into an accordion.

❧ chapter five ❧

THE TRUTH

"**H**elm, I'm coming over."

"Ruth, I've been trying to call you all afternoon. There's been a detective, the detective who was at your house yester . . ."

"I know." Ruth sounded weary, worn out.

"You know?"

"I'll tell all when I get there. Do you have anything to drink?"

"Tea and coffee. Or orange juice."

"I mean alcoholic. Never mind. I'll stop and pick up something."

Helma hung up and hastily finished watering her houseplants. She watered all her plants every four days and cleaned the leaves with a commercial plant cleaner once a month. Some thrived; some died. Those that lingered in plant limbo, Helma placed beside the Bayside Arms dumpster where they promptly disappeared.

She realigned the magazines on her coffee table and put away the dishes in the drainer. Not that Ruth would notice but Helma found it easier to cope with the unknown if there existed around her order and certainty of her own devising. It cleared her mind of mental clutter and heightened her senses. She then stood on her balcony in the cool air, waiting for Ruth and watching the sun sink toward the islands.

Six kayaks followed the rocky shore of the calm bay. Helma had never been in a kayak. The inelegance of the little boats bothered her as did the flip-flopping paddle. It was difficult to take seriously a craft where you reclined in a seat with a back rest, *wearing* your boat.

She idly picked the fading yellow flowers off a pot of daffodils, reminding herself it had also been almost half her life span since she'd paddled a canoe. Maybe paddling wouldn't feel very elegant once she stepped into her old canoe, either.

Ruth wasn't wearing any shade of purple. She entered Helma's apartment in black jeans and a black turtleneck sweater, her hair bushed out the way it generally was when Ruth had been running her hands through it. Unless Ruth had affected a new style, one of her hoop earrings was missing.

She held a brown paper bag crooked under her arm and as she dropped onto Helma's couch she pulled out a bottle of Laphroaig whiskey. The bottle's liquid level was already down two inches. Ruth unscrewed the top and Helma hastily retrieved a juice glass from her cupboard, which Ruth filled to the brim with amber liquid.

"Will you give me a ride home?" Ruth asked.

"You just got here."

"No. I mean when I've unburdened myself and am ready to leave. I'll pick up my car tomorrow." She shook the bottle of whiskey. "You know. Be the designated driver. Save your old friend from a brush with the police." And she laughed so harshly Helma grew uncomfortable.

Helma sat in the rocking chair where she'd placed Detective Carter Houston, facing Ruth. "Ruth, what is happening? Why was that detective asking about you? Where have you been?"

Ruth took a gulp of whiskey from the juice glass and grimaced, squeezing her eyes tight. "That man is definitely not after me for my body."

"Does he think you have some knowledge about the dead man, Joshman Lotz?"

"I don't. Not really. I mean, I didn't know his name. I just saw him. That's all."

"But you didn't say that yesterday morning."

"It didn't seem important at the time."

Helma closed her mouth, exasperated with Ruth's vagaries. She picked up her *Time* magazine and opened it randomly to a story about the health hazards of electric light bulbs.

"Well, don't you want to hear all the gory details?" Ruth demanded.

"If you're actually going to tell me."

"Don't sound like that fussy detecto-bot, Carter Houston. He looks like he stepped out of a Fernando Botero painting, don't you think? Only prissier. Did you notice the way all his orifices seem to pucker?"

Helma bent her head over her magazine again.

"Okay, okay. I'm confessing, see? Thursday night I was in Joker's minding my own business and this greasy old guy started hitting on me." Ruth rolled her eyes. "I ignored him at first. I mean, he was definitely o-l-d, whether he believed it or not. Not that I've got anything against old but this guy would have been a turn-off in his prime."

"The deceased? Joshman Lotz?" Helma asked.

"The deceased. He'd obviously been knocking them back a while 'cause he really got bent when I didn't respond. Started calling me names."

"Like what?"

"He had some winners. I especially liked 'Cunt-zilla.' Another old guy warned him to lay off me and then the two of them got into it so I took the opportunity to leave."

"And that's all?"

"That's all. I don't know how he ended up in my ivy."

"Periwinkle," Helma corrected. "And Detective Houston thinks you know something about Joshman Lotz's death?"

"Who knows? He asked for everything but a urine sample. The same question fifty different ways. Trying to trip me up, I think. What did he ask you?"

"Not much. Whether I knew where you'd been the night before. He inquired about your 'unsettled' lifestyle."

Ruth looked genuinely puzzled. She poured herself more whiskey. "*My* life 'unsettled'? There's nothing unsettled about my life. I paint pictures, recycle, obey the spirit of the law. What's unsettled about that? The twit." Ruth indignantly took another face-grimacing drink.

"Someone at the bar must have told the police about your exchange with Joshman Lotz. Who witnessed it?"

"Everybody there, I guess. The bartender, a couple at a table. Maybe ten or twelve people."

"Who was the man who interfered?"

"I already told you. Another old guy." Ruth tipped her head back toward Helma's ceiling. "The dead man called him Hi-fi, or Stereo, something electric."

"Well, I'm sure this will be the end of it," Helma said. "You were probably just one small step in the police department's standard investigating procedures. They have to explore every possibility. It's what we as taxpayers demand."

"Do you *really* believe that?"

"Yes. Yes, I do," Helma assured Ruth, remembering Detective Carter Houston's smug, tenacious demeanor.

"I wish to hell I knew what was going on," Ruth said. "If only there was somebody—an insider—we could ask."

Ruth leaned forward. She set her glass on the coffee table. Helma quickly slipped a coaster beneath it. "It might leave a mark on the wood," she explained when she saw the way Ruth was looking at her.

"You can do it," Ruth said.

"I already did," Helma said, pointing to the coaster.

"No. *You* can find out what's going on in the hallowed halls of the boys in blue."

"How could I . . ." Helma shook her head. "Whatever

you're thinking, Ruth, I'm not going to do it. The answer is no."

Ruth scooched forward to the edge of the couch. Her voice dropped in entreaty. Cajoling. "You already like the man. There's a spark between you. Anybody with half a hormone can see that. You. Him. No problem. Just invite him over for a dr—cup of tea. Ask him to lunch. Maybe a little walk by the bay? Blink your baby blues a couple of times to soften him up and then just sit back and wait for him to spill the beans. Nothing to it."

"Maybe not for you."

"It would be too obvious if I . . . oh, you're joking. Really, it's a great idea. Simple as pie, Helm."

"Helma," Helma corrected, firmly shaking her head again. "And the answer is still no."

Ruth stuck out her lower lip. "Then how do I know what's going on? How should I act? What if I say the wrong thing?"

"Ruth, you have nothing to worry about. Detective Houston was doing his job, covering all the possibilities. You won't hear from him again and even if you do, just explain whatever you know. There's no possible way you can be implicated in this murder. I'm not going to do anything foolish like attempt to lure information from the chief of police."

Ruth picked up her glass and sat back, slumping into the cushions. "Well, I think it's a missed opportunity for both of us."

They sat silently for a few minutes, neither looking at the other. Finally, Ruth broke the silence. "So how was the funeral? Did Patrice throw herself wailing on the tiny casket and beg to be buried with Binky?"

"She was naturally sorrowful, but Binky *was* a dog, after all."

"I don't know. I've been hurt by a few dogs in my life," Ruth said, her laughter ending in a hiccup. "Speaking of dogs and sorrow, did you do your stint at the crisis center last night?"

Helma shook her head. "I'm taking two months off."

"Too stressful?"

"Sometimes."

Ruth liked to pump Helma about her calls at the crisis center. "Tell me the good stuff," she often said. But Helma guarded the secrets of the crisis line callers as closely as she guarded the questions and reading habits of her library patrons.

The volunteer supervisor had suggested Helma take time off when unaccountably, after successfully and efficiently handling a call from an abused fourteen-year-old girl who'd just slashed her wrists, tears had begun pouring from Helma's eyes. She wasn't sobbing and she was still able to clearly answer the phone and direct the next caller to the mission; she was simply unable to stem the flow of her tears. "It's all right," the supervisor had said, taking Helma's hand. "It happens to all of us. You'll be fine."

Ruth picked up the book on the coffee table that Helma had forgotten to remove. Helma reached for it but she was too late.

"What are you reading?" Ruth asked. She flipped the blue book open to the pages marked with a Flowers of the World bookmark.

Ruth's mouth dropped open. Her face paled. "Holy shit, Helma. I think I'm going to be sick."

"Then close it."

Ruth did and read the book's spine aloud: "*Forensic Physiopathology.*" She stared at Helma, her face still appalled. "Is this some sick new hobby? A little light reading to put you to sleep?"

"It's only shocking at first, until you get used to it. You have to remove yourself from the implications of what you're viewing. I was curious about certain marks around Joshman Lotz's neck. The illustrations in the strangulation chapter are very similar to the condition of his throat, although they'd be easier to compare if they were in color. I wish I'd seen his entire neck." Helma held out her hand for the book. "Frequently, in a garroted-type death, there's a gap . . . "

"Not another word, Helma Zukas. This is why we have police detectives and coroners and stuff, so *we* don't have to think about it. Where'd you get this?"

"From the library."

"It was right there for God or anybody to pluck off the shelf?"

"It was in closed stacks."

"Well, that renews my faith in libraries. I'd give a nine-year-old a sex manual before I'd give him this." She took the book back from Helma, opened it two inches wide, leaned over, and peeked inside. "Oh, gross!"

"Page 318 is the worst," Helma warned her. "Don't look."

Ruth turned to page 318, holding the book as far from herself as she could. "That's impossible!" She flipped a few more pages and turned the book toward Helma. "Did you see *this* one?"

Helma's phone and doorbell rang at the same time. Ruth slammed the forensic pathology book closed and stood, a little unsteadily. "You get the phone. I'll get the door, oh popular one."

It was Helma's brother Bruce on the phone and Walter David at the door. Helma happily turned her back on Ruth and Walter David and concentrated on her conversation with Bruce.

"It's all set, Helma," Bruce told her, "but I thought I'd check with you one more time before I actually shipped it out."

"Is there a problem?"

"No. Not for me, anyway. You're the one getting stuck with the bill. It's cheaper to ship a body than a fifteen-foot canoe."

"Fourteen feet, nine inches. But they can do it?"

"Yeah. You'll have to pick it up at air freight in Belle-haven, though. It's going out Monday morning and will arrive on Tuesday. Do you want me to send your paddles?"

Uncle Tony had made the paddles, too, carving the grips to fit her hand. There were two paddles, a longer one Helma normally used and a shorter one, her bow paddle. "Are they all right?" she asked Bruce.

"The bow paddle's warped. They need reoiling but they're okay."

Behind Helma, Ruth and Walter David laughed. Helma covered her ear with her hand. "Send them, then."

"I'd forgotten how beautiful Uncle Tony's canoes were," Bruce continued wistfully. "Wish I hadn't been so stupid as to sell mine. The boys would have loved it. I hear voices. Are you having a party?"

"No, it's just Ruth talking to the building manager."

"Ruth Winthrop? That's almost a party. Tell her hi for me. Mom doing okay?"

"She seems to be. She took on a hiking club after her romance cooled off and has been even more active than usual. I think she's dating."

"Good for her. I'll bet Dad's spinning."

"How's your sculpture?" Helma asked.

Lately, Bruce's work had consisted of stylized carvings of Lithuanian shrines and figures that he sold to nostalgic rich Lithuanians and collectors in Chicago and Massachusetts, once even sending a shipment to Lithuania itself.

"I'm doing a *Rupintojelis*—the Sorrowful Man—series right now. Getting a little tired of it but it's all been commissioned so I'm committed."

When Helma hung up, Ruth was smiling, one arm through Walter David's, who looked a little dazed.

"Walter's taking me home on his motorcycle so you are hereby relieved of your civic duties. Whoops. I forgot my whiskey."

Walter David grinned uncertainly at Helma. Tooth marks from a comb shone in his hair. "I didn't mean to interrupt. Is this okay?"

"Certainly. Thank you for returning my slipper."

Walter David actually blushed. Helma had never seen him act so . . . adolescent. It had to be Ruth's influence.

"I saw it fall off the balcony. I didn't . . ."

"I'm ready," Ruth interrupted. "See ya, Helm. Don't forget that other matter we talked about. One little call is all it takes."

"Goodbye, Ruth. I don't believe any further action will be necessary."

Helma closed her door and covered *Forensic Physiopathology* with her *Time* magazine. She removed Ruth's juice glass from the coffee table, her nose twitching at the smell. She had no intention of calling Chief of Police Wayne Gallant just to elicit details on a standard police procedure. There was simply no need to whatsoever.

❧ chapter six ❧

THE WHOLE TRUTH

Sunday morning, when Helma returned from eight-thirty Mass and a stop at the newly opened Pacific Bakery to purchase a plain croissant, she found Ruth slumped on the third-floor landing of the Bayside Arms with Boy Cat Zukas draped across her legs like a secondhand fur piece.

Ruth wore the same clothes she'd worn Saturday, only more wrinkled, the sweater bagging. Black eye makeup had spread to her left cheekbone.

"I'm in trouble," Ruth said, no trace of humor lightening her voice, her face drawn. Helma believed her.

"Why don't you come inside?" Helma asked.

Ruth nodded, half rose, then held up an unprotesting Boy Cat Zukas by the front legs and kissed him between the eyes.

"He can't come in," Helma said.

"I know that. He knows that. So why say it?"

Ruth smelled of old whiskey. She stood in front of Helma's balcony door, staring out to sea, her hands clasped behind her back. Helma set the white box holding her croissant on the kitchen counter and waited.

Without turning, Ruth finally spoke in a heavy voice. "The police searched my house this morning. They had a search warrant."

Helma was so shocked she sat on the arm of her couch. "Ruth! What were they looking for?"

"The murder weapon used to kill Joshman Lotz."

Helma closed her mouth, trying to sort out these latest developments. A search warrant. Search warrants weren't issued unless there was probable cause, were they?

"The police suspect that you . . ." she began.

"That's right."

"With what reason, Ruth? It doesn't make any sense."

Ruth finally turned around, her eyes dull, rubbing her arms. "It's like this. You know how easily old people bruise? It seems there's a bruise on the dead guy's left upper arm that sort of matches my hand print."

"But you didn't touch him."

Ruth bit her lip. "Well, actually. Yes, I did. He started to follow me out of the bar and I turned around and grabbed him by the arm and told him . . . " She shrugged apologetically at Helma. "A witness swore I said, 'Bugger off you dried-up old fart or I'll wrap your balls around your neck.' "

"And he was strangled."

"But obviously not with his balls, or there wouldn't have been any reason to search my house."

"Was Detective Houston part of the search?"

"The instigator, was my impression. He was snuffling around like an overfed bloodhound. He also suggested I stick close to home for a while."

"You're not a suspect, are you?"

"I haven't been *officially* informed I am, but I do sound like a 'person of interest,' don't you think?"

"Yes," Helma agreed. "You do. Did they find anything in your house?"

"God, Helm. What are you suggesting? I *didn't* kill the guy. What could they find? I don't even remember threatening him." She thought for a few moments. "But that was a pretty good line. It sounds like something I'd say, doesn't it?"

"Actually, it does," Helma concurred. The police be-

lieved Ruth was involved in the murder. They'd
searched her house. Her handprint matched bruises on
the dead man's arm. "Did you tell the detective the reason your handprint matched the bruises?"

"Yeah. You should have seen his face light up."

"But Chief Gallant wasn't there?"

"He only puts in an appearance when you're around."

"But there must be other suspects."

"If there are, nobody shared that little item with me.
I'm tailor-made, aren't I? I have a teensy altercation with
the fellow, threaten him, and he shows up dead in my
periwinkle with my mitts all over him."

"Or someone thought you'd be the perfect suspect and
took advantage of your quarrel to make you appear responsible."

"I did overhear one tidbit," Ruth said. "One of the
cops, that guy with the mole? He picked up a wooden
easel I had folded in the corner of my bathroom. I heard
him say, 'This is about the right size.'"

"But he didn't say what it was the right size for?"

"Uh-uh. He kinda hefted it and then another cop said
it was too thick."

"Too thick," Helma mused. "There must have been
another injury to Lotz besides the strangulation."

"In addition to my bruising his delicate skin?"

"It could be. Maybe on his body where I couldn't see
it. Are you certain you didn't know anyone else in the
bar?"

"By sight, maybe. And Kipper, the bartender."

"We'd better talk to him," Helma said, ignoring the
way Ruth's eyebrows suddenly raised in hope. "Someone else may know about a quarrel or motive toward
Joshman Lotz."

"Won't you quiz the chief and see what's going on,
like we talked about? I can't be their only suspect."

"I already said no," Helma told her, rising from the
arm of the couch and moving to sit on the cushion.

Ruth's chin came up. "I'm not totally without re-
sources, you know. If you won't do it, I will. Maybe I'll

even talk to your chief of police myself. Put in a good word for you while I'm quizzing him."

"That's *not* a good idea, Ruth. Besides, don't you think meddling would call more attention to yourself?"

"Meddle in *what*? It's my life we're talking about here. My reputation. You don't have to stir your stumps for me but I intend to get to the bottom of this mess."

Helma traced her finger slowly around the face of her watch, matching speed with the second hand, picturing Ruth confronting Wayne Gallant. Anything could come out of Ruth's mouth.

"You didn't tell me all the facts of the matter the first time, Ruth," Helma said. "Is there anything else you've left out?"

Ruth earnestly held up her right hand. "No. I swear it. Will you talk to the chief?"

"I have to think about it."

Ruth got up and reached for Helma's phone. "Let's call him now."

"I said I have to think about it."

"Sorry. How long do you need to think? An hour? Twenty minutes?"

"Ruth."

"What time is it?" Ruth asked.

"Ten-thirty."

Ruth's face softened. "Guess I'll go home then. Paul's going to call around noon."

Paul lived in Minnesota and for over a year Ruth had been carrying on an unlikely long-distance relationship with him. Unlikely because it had gone on for so long and also because Ruth acted as irritated by the relationship as she was drawn to it. "He's not my type," she'd said more than once. "Definitely."

Helma watched Ruth climb into her car and drive away. Not more than five seconds later a plain blue sedan Helma hadn't noticed anyone get into, pulled away from the shoulder of the boulevard and followed after Ruth.

Helma rubbed her temples, feeling a knotty pressure

building from holding back speculation. She returned to her living room and picked up the Smithsonian magazine with its neatly scalpeled cumulus clouds, contemplating the skill and concentration it would require to cut out the fully leafed oak tree in the foreground. She set it down again. No, there was a folder full of trees, all sizes and species, in her file cabinet in the hallway.

She filled a glass with water and drank it in front of her picture window, remembering a curious quote of Thomas Wolfe's she'd found for a patron. "We are fixed and certain," he'd written, "only when we are in motion." With goals, intent on accomplishment or purpose. And literally, too, Helma thought, considering how much easier it was for her to tamp down worries and solve complicated problems while in motion, while walking or driving.

A breeze riffled the brightly striped windsock on Mrs. Whitney's balcony. The day was overcast but not too cool, perfect for a brisk walk. Helma changed from her Sunday dress to slacks and sturdy shoes. She pinned her house key inside her pants pocket and left her apartment, within moments striding in long, fluid steps, back straight, arms swinging, head high, refusing to permit murders, investigations, or Chief Wayne Gallant into her thoughts.

Trees along the boulevard were in blossom: cherries, flowering crabapple, magnolia. Petals drifted loose when the breeze rose.

Helma entered Boardwalk City Park from above, descending a timbered staircase from the boulevard to the lush crescent-shaped grounds so low to the bay she'd actually seen the park flood once during an exceptionally high tide. The tide was normal today, turning back to sea, leaving behind tangles of seaweed along the glossy black rocks.

Helma picked up a crumpled paper cup near the playground and carried it to the nearest trash can. A lone crabber on the boardwalk drew in a crab pot, empty except for a chicken neck.

It was during her second circuit of the graveled path edging the park that Helma noticed the boisterous group gathered around a barbecue between two picnic tables. The smoky odor of grilling beef filled the east end of the park. A woman detached herself from the group and waved.

"Helma!"

Obviously Roger Barnhard wasn't the only ex-spouse who'd taken up physical activity. At first Helma didn't recognize the children's librarian's ex-wife in this slender, more muscular, and yes, younger-appearing version, her hair back in a ponytail, wearing green spandex shorts, hiking boots, and a stylishly outdoorsy parka.

"Hello, Connie."

"Care to join us for hamburgers? There's plenty."

"I don't want to intrude."

Connie didn't argue.

"How are your children?" Helma asked. She didn't know Connie personally, had only seen her at library functions where, taller than her ex-husband, she'd remained in the background, not contributing much, seeming to be more shy than unfriendly.

"Great. They're with Roger tonight, at a movie or something." She paused, then asked too casually, "Do you talk to Roger very much?"

"Only on a professional basis," Helma told her.

"Mmm. I heard you were going to canoe on the library's team in the Snow to Surf Race."

"I've been invited, that's all. I haven't decided yet."

Connie raised her arms, making exaggerated muscles. "I'm on the planning department's team. Our team and the library's are competing in the same division, how about that? That's what this barbecue's about. We're supposed to be building team spirit." She grinned. "Although I think a few people in the department would *love* to compete against each other. To the death."

"Which leg will you be doing?" Helma asked.

"The mountain bike." Connie shifted from the ball of one foot to the other like she might sprint off.

"So's Roger."

"I know. Isn't it cute? Those mountain bikes sat gathering spider webs in our garage until we split up." Connie motioned to two men drinking beer by the barbecue. "Come here, you guys. Meet your competition."

The two men, both blond, one in a t-shirt with the bottom cut off exposing his navel, and the other in slacks and an alligator-decorated polo shirt, joined them.

"This is Helma Zukas," Connie said. "She might do the library's canoe leg."

"Yeah?" the one with the navel said, without a great show of interest.

The other one looked at Helma as if he were about to indulgently pat her head. "Well, good luck to you," he said unconvincingly. "We'll be at the finish line cheering when you come in."

"Oh, Al," Connie said. "Don't listen to him, Helma. I'm sure the library will put up a good fight."

"I'm sure we . . . they, that is, will," Helma said.

And there was nothing else to say. The two men returned to the barbecue, sharing a glance and a laugh, and Connie said, "Will you do me a favor?"

"If I can."

"Will you tell Roger I looked really good?"

"If he should ask me, I certainly will," Helma told her sincerely.

Back in her apartment, Helma fixed herself a cup of tea and outlined her invitation to Chief Gallant on a piece of notepaper. Ruth was erroneous in believing there was anything more than professional courtesy between Helma and the chief. A mutual respect and totally understandable admiration for each other's professional careers, that was all. And discussing a murder involving her friend was completely natural. *Not* discussing it would be unnatural.

When her tea was gone and her cup cool to the touch, Helma reached for her phone. It wasn't necessary to look up Chief Gallant's personal phone number, the unlisted number he'd given her two years ago. She'd called it twice since then but for some unaccountable reason, the phone number had remained in her memory, as did many phone numbers, including her mother's, Serena who cut her hair, and the circulation department of the *Bellehaven Daily News*.

She rhythmically breathed while she dialed the number. Inhale for four, hold for four, exhale for eight.

He answered on the second ring.

"May I speak with Chief Gallant, please," she said, recognizing his voice.

"Speaking."

"This is Helma Zukas from the Bellehaven Public Library."

"Helma, you're not working today, are you?"

"No. I'm at home. I'd like to invite you to have lunch with me tomorrow, Tuesday, or Wednesday, whichever is most convenient for you."

"Well, thank you. Tuesday I have a lunch meeting but how about tomorrow? Do you have somewhere in mind?"

Helma didn't. Not Saul's Deli. There was sure to be someone from the library eating lunch there, or maybe even her mother. It had to be more distant, less conspicuous.

"Sam and Ella's?" she suggested, naming a restaurant where no one she knew ever ate. It had managed to remain open for years despite there rarely being more than three or four cars in the parking lot at a time.

"Sam and Ella's," he agreed. "Shall I pick you up?"

"I'll meet you there at noon."

"Fine. I'm looking forward to it."

Helma hung up, wiped her palms on her skirt, and headed for her bedroom to inspect her closet.

🌿 chapter seven 🌿

MONDAY ADVANCES

On Monday morning, Patrice, once more perfectly coiffed and postured, lips slightly pursed and glasses hanging from a gold chain on her bosom, was seated vigilantly at her desk when the rest of the staff arrived. The only indication of her recent loss was an unconcealable puffiness around her eyes and two new framed photographs of Binky joining the three already on her desk.

"Good morning, Helma," she said formally. "Your presence on Saturday was appreciated."

"You're welcome. It was a moving event," Helma responded just as formally." And your gardens are truly beautiful," she added with sincerity.

"I've always believed that contributing beauty to the world furthers the evolutionary process of mankind," Patrice pronounced.

"Yeah, I loved those frizzy blue things," Eve said. She handed Helma a folded sheet of paper.

"What's this?"

"Official Snow to Surf rules. Every participant gets a copy. Who's your canoe partner? Do you have somebody in mind or should we ask around the library?"

"Speaking of friends," George Melville interrupted, "I

67

saw in yesterday's rag that the guy in your friend Ruth's alley didn't just keel over of natural causes; he was murdered. You still say you're not involved?"

"Of course I'm not involved."

"You mean the Lotz guy?" Eve asked. "My grandfather knew him years ago. He said he was a real lowlife."

"Your grandfather's correct," Patrice said, standing and speaking over the shelves that separated her cubicle from Helma's. "Joshman Lotz was a bounder and I doubt he'll be much missed."

"What's a 'bounder?' " Eve asked.

"There's a fine, overly-expensive, underused dictionary on the dictionary stand," George Melville told her. "Look it up."

Eve wrinkled her nose at George. "I bet it's like 'lowlife.' "

Helma listened attentively. "Why was he disliked, I wonder," she said, glancing from Eve to Patrice.

"Grandpa said if you walked past Joshman Lotz, you'd better check your pockets afterward."

"What *I* know," Patrice said, dropping her voice to her favorite conspiratorial tone, her tired eyes brightening and her nostrils flaring as if she'd caught a whiff of a deliciously delicate scent, "is that he was married to one of my schoolmates over forty years ago. My Aunt Julia claimed he had a roving eye, and," Patrice glanced from face to face meaningfully, "the rumor was he didn't treat poor Alice very well."

"What happened to Alice?" Helma asked Patrice, trying not to appear overly interested.

"She died after childbirth complications," Patrice said. "She was only in her mid-twenties."

"Did the baby die, too?" Eve asked, her eyes already tearing up.

"Lotz turned it over for adoption. I wasn't living here at the time but I remember my mother saying Alice's mother wanted the baby but she was too old and there was bad blood between her and Lotz anyway. It was quite the scandal." Patrice's forehead wrinkled. "He'd be in his late thirties now."

"Maybe he never forgave his father and came back to seek his revenge," Eve suggested dramatically.

"It was probably a closed adoption, " Patrice said.

"People can break those," Eve said."I saw a story on TV about a woman who found her real mother through dreams."

Roberta pushed a book truck past which held a single volume of *Burke's Peerage*, reels of microfilm from interlibrary loan, and a stack of books containing Virginia will, military, marriage, birth, and death records. "Mrs. Boniface has finally traced her lineage back to 1758," she told them wearily. "Fortunately, on the revolutionary side. It was doubtful for a while."

"So she's busily filing for her DAR membership?" George asked.

"She's been carrying a stamped, addressed envelope with her for six months."

The conversation regarding Joshman Lotz was at an end. Patrice disappeared into her own cubicle. George followed Roberta to hers.

"Oh, yeah, Helma," Eve said."There's a Snow to Surf strategy meeting at noon today."

"I have a previous engagement," Helma told her.

"Can't you break it?"

"No. I can't. Besides, I haven't decided whether to participate or not."

Eve's mouth opened in surprise. "You have to, Helma. We're counting on you. Otherwise, we're sunk."

"I'll decide by Friday, Eve. That's all I can promise at this time."

Eve glumly departed and Helma sat in her desk chair, but not before she glimpsed Patrice, elbows on her desk, chin in palm, staring at her framed pictures of Binky.

On her way to the library that morning, Helma had stopped at the "Half-Time" twenty-four-hour grocery store. In the school supplies aisle she'd chosen a small blue spiral notebook, similar to but less imposing than Chief Gallant's.

Now she opened it to the second clean page, wrote

"J. Lotz" on the top line and quickly jotted down the pertinent information from her conversations with Mrs. Whitney, Eve, and Patrice. Then, using yellow Post-It notes as tabs, she divided the notebook into five sections, labeling each one: J. Lotz, Witnesses, Ruth, Police, and Misc. Under "Police," she included Detective Carter Houston, but under "Ruth" she described the search warrant. When she was finished, Helma slipped the notebook into her purse next to her checkbook and glanced at her watch. There were still three hours until her lunch appointment.

Ms. Moon stopped by Patrice's desk. Helma didn't intend to listen but in the cramped workroom it was impossible not to.

"What is this?" Patrice asked in indignation.

"The date you'll be chaperoning the children's overnighter in the library. We're calling them, 'Camp-out in a Book.' Isn't that clever?"

"Not particularly. And I have no intention of chaperoning children. Find someone else." Patrice's voice rang with angry abandon.

"Patrice," Ms. Moon cooed. "We're all taking turns . . ."

"I'm not," Patrice snapped.

Helma listened with admiration. Ms. Moon spluttered gently, then clucked and tut-tutted. "You're still grieving, Patrice," she said softly. "We'll discuss it later."

"I won't discuss it now or later. I will not chaperone children's activities. I'm a librarian, not a day-care employee."

At ten o'clock, Helma took over an hour of George Melville's reference desk time so George could attend a joint workshop titled 'Cataloging: Cornerstone or Buggy Whip?' at the local college.

"Excuse me, Miss Zukas."

Helma raised her head from the manual for the CD-ROM version of the *Oxford English Dictionary*, thinking that sometimes simply knowing your alphabet and turning the pages of a printed book couldn't be improved on for efficiency, to a middle-aged man she recognized as one of her "regulars," a patron who expressly asked for her or timed his visits to her desk schedule. He'd confided his name was "Rock, like Rock Hudson," although there was no resemblance in this narrow-shouldered, thin-haired man. None at all.

Over the past year Helma had helped him find study materials for various careers and positions: policeman, fireman, postal employee, hotel management, all of which he'd failed, he told Helma, due to circumstances beyond his control, like bad lighting and reverse discrimination.

"How may I help you?" she asked, bracing herself for what was sure to be an involved story.

But today Rock was all business. "I need some information on locksmithing," he said, squeezing his nose between thumb and forefinger. "I'm applying for a security guard position."

"In the 680's," Helma told him. She keyed in the subject on the reference desk computer. "683.32 to be exact."

"Thank you, ma'am," he fairly saluted and marched away toward the nonfiction stacks.

At 11:50, Helma left the library and drove across town to Sam and Ella's. The low restaurant sat on a busy corner, next to a shopping center. Bright red and white awnings hung out over the sidewalk all the way around the building, which Helma hoped would cut the sounds and sights of traffic. Only two cars sat in the lot beside the building and neither looked like it belonged to a policeman so Helma drove around the block twice more until she saw a plain dark sedan had joined the other two vehicles.

The interior of Sam and Ella's was determinedly Italian: red and white and green, accented by artificial vines, bunches of grapes, and squat wine bottles.

A lone elderly man sat at a table near the door eating a plate of spaghetti and reading a folded newspaper. At the far end of the restaurant the chief was already seated beside a window too shaded by the awning to see the street—or to be seen. He stood as Helma approached the table, smiling, holding out his hand. She took it, expecting a handshake, but he covered hers with both his own, dwarfing it between his two big warm hands, bending over her a little. "This was a good idea, Helma," he said. His eyes crinkled. He motioned her to the chair opposite him.

Helma's hello came out in a squeak he didn't seem to notice. She sat down and placed her purse beneath her chair, hooking the strap around the chair leg.

"Have you eaten here before?" he asked.

"No, but I've heard . . . well, to be honest, I haven't heard anything."

Wayne Gallant laughed and held up the menu. "It looks like we're on our own. That's a beautiful pin. My grandmother had one similar."

Helma touched the cameo at her throat. "This belonged to my grandmother."

"There's a coincidence." He smiled and suddenly Helma was at ease. She returned his smile, wondering why she'd been nervous about their lunch date.

They chatted about the effects of the new mall, the juvenile crime rate, and Bellehaven's growth and had already ordered lunch before Helma was able to work the conversation around to the murder of Joshman Lotz.

"Are you having any success with your investigation of the Lotz murder?" she asked.

Helma didn't see why, but Chief Gallant set down his water glass and looked at her, one corner of his mouth rising. "Not unqualified success."

"Detective Houston questioned both Ruth and me."

"That's standard procedure."

"I learned an interesting fact this morning," she said. "Did you know Joshman Lotz put his own infant child up for adoption after his wife died?"

"He was married three times," the chief said. "All three women are dead."

"This would have been thirty-some years ago. He was married to a classmate of a library employee."

Chief Gallant didn't appear surprised or, actually, even that interested. He nodded politely.

Over the chief's shoulder, Helma saw their waiter standing in the kitchen doorway. He stepped back into the kitchen, leaving the door swinging. Helma caught a quick glimpse of three more men inside, quietly engaged in conversation.

"Are you investigating Joshman Lotz's past?" Helma asked the chief.

"It's a component of the investigation."

"It may have more bearing on his death than the present or near past. Perhaps revenge or unfinished family matters."

They paused while the waiter set salads in front of them. "Excuse me, sir," the waiter apologized after clumsily tipping the chief's plate so a cherry tomato rolled onto the table. The waiter caught the tomato at the edge of the table. "I'll bring you a fresh one."

"No need," Chief Gallant told him.

When the waiter was gone, Helma said, "You seem to make our waiter nervous."

"Why do you say that?"

"His clumsiness. I saw him watching you from the kitchen."

The chief dashed extra salt and pepper on his salad and looked thoughtfully after the waiter. "Police tend to do that to people."

He leaned across the table. "Do you have information concerning Joshman Lotz's past you'd like to share with the police?"

"Only rumors," she admitted.

"I see."

Helma stiffened at his tone. "On the other hand, I *know* Ruth Winthrop and I'm positive she had nothing to do with his death."

"There's enough circumstantial evidence for us to be interested in Miss Winthrop," he said.

"Such as?" she asked.

"Haven't we been through this type of conversation

before, Helma? You know police information is confidential."

"What about the murder weapon?" Helma asked as she cut her tomato into four equal quarters. "You didn't find anything in Ruth's house that matched the marks around Lotz's throat, did you?"

"It sounds like you had ample time to examine the body."

"It wouldn't take an observant person more than an instant to see those marks."

"And we already know you're observant."

"Observant enough to notice you're having Ruth followed."

"As I explained, she's of interest to our investigation."

"So by extension, I must be, too." Another waiter peeked out through the kitchen door and Helma lowered her voice. "I saw the body before the police did. Ruth and I are friends. We see each other fairly often."

Chief Gallant thoughtfully chewed a lettuce leaf. "It might be wise to see a little less of Ruth Winthrop during our investigation."

Helma set down her fork. "What are you implying?"

"Only that it's unwise to entangle yourself in a police matter."

"So I should walk away and leave a friend at the mercy of your department?"

The chief set aside his empty salad plate. "Of course not, but also you shouldn't hinder the police. You may inadvertently tamper with important evidence."

"And how could I possibly do that?"

"Helma, in the past you've had the tendency to be . . . well . . . independent."

Helma couldn't restrain the tinge of smugness that crept into her voice. "And hasn't my 'independence' helped clear up certain nasty police matters?"

"So far. But only at great danger to yourself and others."

Yet another waiter delivered their entrees: a turkey and havarti sandwich for Helma and a dish called "meatball mania" for Chief Gallant. Helma checked her sandwich to be sure there wasn't any mustard on it and after sending the waiter to fetch her a fresher pat of butter, she said, "It's curious that this restaurant has more employees than customers, isn't it?"

Wayne Gallant stilled, his head tipped. Two lines appeared between his eyes.

"There seems to be quite a large kitchen staff as well," Helma added.

"Evening is probably their prime business period."

Helma waited a moment, then asked, guessing, "What about the mark on Lotz's body as if someone had swung a board at him?"

"How did you know about that?" the chief asked, his eyes so penetrating, his voice suddenly gone so cold, Helma could only tell the truth.

"Ruth overheard two policemen talking in her house."

Chief Gallant's face went blank. Someone was in trouble for speaking too freely and Helma had done it.

Helma took two more bites of her sandwich and a sip of tea before she asked, "Have you questioned the bartender?"

"He's given some testimony."

"Did he tell you about Lotz's friend Stereo?" Helma asked, carefully watching Chief Gallant's face.

"You mean Radio . . ." The chief stopped, a forkful of pasta and meatballs halfway to his mouth. "I believe you just tricked a piece of information from me, Helma Zukas."

Helma ducked her head. "I confused his name, that's all. But this 'Radio' also quarreled with Lotz the night he died. He might have more information than Ruth."

"Mmm. This pasta's a little salty. How's your sandwich?"

And that was the only piece of new information Helma was able to draw from the chief. They chatted amiably and suddenly it was time for Helma to return to the library.

"How many waiters do you have?" the chief asked the curly haired girl at the cash register.

"It depends on how busy we are. Sometimes two or three. Sometimes one."

Helma turned away in embarrassment as the chief removed a toothpick from the plastic dispenser beside the cash register.

In the parking lot, Helma unlocked her car door and the chief opened it for her. "Helma," he said, bending down to eye level as she buckled her seat belt, "it wasn't necessary to invite me to lunch to pump me for information. I would have told you the same thing over the phone."

Helma blushed, at a loss for words.

"And also," he continued, "I would have been honored to have lunch with you without subterfuge, just for the pleasure of your company."

He placed the toothpick between his teeth and got into his car, waving jauntily at Helma as he pulled onto the busy street.

Ruth sat on the bookmobile's loading dock, in animated conversation with Jack the janitor. She rose when Helma turned into the library lot and was beside the Buick before Helma could set her parking brake.

"What'd he say?" Ruth demanded. She had recovered enough from her weekend ordeal with Detective Carter Houston to be back in purple.

"Nothing we don't already know except that Lotz's friend in the bar who came to your defense was named 'Radio.' "

"Radio What?"

"That's all he would tell me. Otherwise, you're 'of interest.' " Helma glanced into the street, searching for a plain police car. A woman stood by a parking meter with her collie. An elderly man sat on a bench reading a book to two redheaded children. No one else seemed to be suspiciously pausing or waiting near the library.

"Well, then tonight we have to talk to Kipper, the bartender at Joker's. Pick me up at seven-thirty, okay?"

"I don't think that's wise, Ruth. Let the police do the questioning."

Ruth shrugged indifferently. "If you don't want to go, I'll go alone."

Helma had no doubt Ruth would, and who knew what mischief would follow. What would Ruth's surveillance team make of Ruth returning to the scene of her meeting with Lotz?

"All right," Helma told her. "I'll pick you up." She'd think of an excuse to forestall Ruth's "talk" with the bartender once Ruth was safely in her car.

On Helma's desk sat a box of chocolates. "Please say yes to the Library Snow to Surf team," the accompanying note said, graced with a sticker of a red heart punctured by an arrow. Helma raised her head and peered around the workroom. Eve stood next to George Melville, both of them smiling hopefully.

❧ chapter eight ❧

ROSE TRAIL

"**H**ow long do you intend to wear those colors?" Helma asked when Ruth had settled into the passenger seat and Helma was steering through the alley, avoiding the deceptively shallow puddles.

Ruth turned her purple-shadowed eyes toward Helma. A sprig of lilac was tucked behind her ear. "Artistic expression isn't concerned with temporal time. One phase naturally evolves into another. Why? Is violet too passionate for your tastes?"

"It can be an annoying color."

"A color, 'annoying'?" Ruth asked, frowning. "Do you remember Dubakas's house back in dear old Scoop River?"

Helma did. The bright purple house by the river, with pale lilac trim and purple curtains in the window and purple bird feeders in the yard. "And his fence?"

"Half-buried tires painted purple," Ruth supplied. "I wonder if it's still there?"

Helma shook her head. "Aunt Em said downstaters bought the land and replaced the house with a double-wide trailer."

"I submit to you, Helma, which house is the more interesting?"

"You're assigning a positive value to the term, 'interesting,' Ruth. I don't believe that's etymologically correct. To be 'interesting' only means to hold the attention."

"That's what I said."

Helma stopped at the cross street onto the boulevard, put her car in neutral, and said to Ruth, "The new Clint Eastwood movie opened at the Grand Cinema," she said. "If we hurry we could just make it. I'll treat."

"Since when did you become a Clint Eastwood fan?"

Helma shrugged. She'd never seen a Clint Eastwood movie. "I know he's one of your favorite actors."

"I do believe you're trying to deter me from my mission at Joker's."

"To be honest, I am."

"Sorry. You're too late."

Helma gave up and turned onto the boulevard, heading toward the older, more touristy section of Bellehaven. The pavement was shiny wet and, ahead of them, the brick buildings glowed red. Once this district of town had vainly hoped to be a nineteenth-century boom town; now its historic old buildings mainly held coffeehouses, restaurants, galleries, and the best bookstore in Bellehaven.

"If we do this, Ruth," Helma warned, "we have to choose our words carefully."

"What do you mean, 'if'?"

"I'm reminding you that anything we say or ask will probably be remembered . . ."

" 'And may be used against us later in a court of law,' " Ruth quoted. "Is that what you mean?"

"Well, yes."

"So you're telling me not to shoot off my mouth?"

"To use discretion."

"Huh," Ruth grunted. "With you to watch over me, how could I possibly slip up?"

Helma glanced in her rearview mirror as she turned the corner toward Joker's. The next two cars behind her kept on driving, but the third, a dark sedan, turned behind them. Helma sighed.

"There's a parking spot, right next to that van," Ruth said. "We should have brought a tape recorder or something."

"I have a notebook," Helma said, showing Ruth the blue spiral notebook.

"Are you taking sleuthing lessons from our chief of police and his band of merry men?"

"I'm always open to learning new skills," Helma told her.

It was the first time Helma had been inside Joker's. She rarely entered establishments that concentrated on selling alcoholic beverages and she was pleasantly surprised by the rich wood bar, the soft lighting, and the clean floors. Eight or nine well-behaved people sat in the bar, sipping drinks and talking.

The bartender, a bearded man who had to lean down or his head was distorted behind rows of hanging glasses, nodded to them.

"Hi, Kipper," Ruth said, sitting at a bar stool. Helma stood uncertainly, looking longingly at a table against the wall.

"C'mon, Helma." Ruth patted the stool next to her.

Helma reluctantly climbed onto the stool, stepping on one of its lower rungs to reach the seat. She folded her hands over her purse on her lap, glancing around the room from the corners of her eyes to see if they were being watched with undue interest. But no, the couple in the corner only saw one another. Three young people, who Helma doubted were over twenty-one, were engrossed in a board game with black and white stones. A woman sat alone staring into her glass, and a middle-aged couple laughed together on the other side of the room. Ruth and Helma were the only customers seated at the bar.

"Has Radio been in yet tonight?" Ruth asked, daintily sipping from a shot glass of whiskey. Helma drank a glass of Diet 7-Up.

"Haven't seen him," Kipper replied. Guardedly, Helma thought.

"It's okay," Ruth said, smiling so warmly Kipper the bartender took a step closer to her, as if drawn by a magnet. "That chubby detective? He told me he'd talked to you and Radio. I'm cleared, off the hook, free as a bird."

"Then they know who did it?" Kipper asked. "Radio's aching to go after whoever killed Josh."

Helma considered the complexity of her 7-Up bubbles as Ruth blithely said, "The chief told me they'll be making an arrest in the next couple of days. Some old buddy of Lotz's." She put her finger to her lips. "Just between you and us."

"From prison?" Kipper asked. "Radio said Josh made some enemies inside."

Ruth nudged Helma with her knee, as if Helma weren't already listening. "Maybe," Ruth said in admirable blandness. "He was lucky to get out as soon as he did."

Kipper snorted. "Twelve years, when his original sentence was ten? Not too lucky if you ask me."

Ruth's eyes sparkled. She settled on her seat, wiggling her bottom and slouching forward onto her elbows. She was about to step beyond discretion and give herself away. Helma knew the signs.

"I believe that man's trying to attract your attention," Helma told Kipper, pointing to the middle-aged couple across the room.

"Thanks."

"What'd you do that for?" Ruth asked. "I was just getting hot."

"I don't believe he could tell us much more."

"I get it," Ruth said, pointing her finger at Helma. "You thought I was about to do the 'shooting off my mouth' thing, right?"

"It crossed my mind."

"What are you, the thought patrol?"

"The police will probably question him about this conversation so I recommend against becoming too confidential."

"The police? How will they know we were here, or that we even talked to Kipper?"

"I believe they already know. A dark car followed us from your house."

"Geez. If those guys are serious about being invisible, why don't they drive minivans or Hondas or something?" Ruth turned her bar stool until she could lean her back against the bar. "So what do we do now?"

"It depends. We could go home. We could drive over to Sunspot Acres where I suspect your Mr. Radio also lives and let the police tag along behind us."

"Or?" Ruth asked.

Helma turned on her bar stool, too. "Personally, I feel uncomfortable when I'm being followed. The rain's stopped. We might walk the Rose Trail."

"You mean that trail that passes by the back door of this bar and meanders near Sunspot Acres?"

"It's not that far."

"You're a genius, Helma."

"Thank you," Helma acknowledged.

Without calling attention to themselves, they departed through the back door of Joker's, loudly opening and closing the women's restroom door as they passed it, Helma leading the way. The Rose Trail wound between brick buildings where cobblestone sidewalks were lit by glowing lamps on Victorian lampposts, along narrow alleys and through a deep ravine lined with wild roses that passed beneath the main street, skirting a small creek.

"My legs aren't as long as yours," Helma reminded Ruth as the trail veered from the alley into the trees.

"Sorry," Ruth said, shortening her stride. "How long do you think we've been followed?"

"*We've* been followed since I picked you up but I think *you've* been under surveillance at least since your house was searched."

"God, I hope I've made it worth their time."

Under lamplight by the little creek, a toddler in a yellow slicker and his father set sail paper boats decorated by crayons, too intent to notice Ruth and Helma. They reminded Helma of her canoe, due to arrive at the Belle-haven airport Tuesday afternoon. It was already somewhere between Michigan and Washington, packed so well, Bruce had promised, 'a raw egg wouldn't break.'

"How much room do you have in your garage?" she asked Ruth.

"Room for my car and some junk. Why?"

"Are there rafters?"

"I guess so. Is there someone you care to hang?"

"Bruce is shipping out my canoe. It should get here tomorrow and I need a place to store it."

Ruth stopped and regarded Helma. "Your *canoe*? One of the famous family canoes? What for?"

Helma couldn't bring herself to mention the Snow to Surf Race. Not yet. "Just to have. I might do a little canoeing. Paddling is excellent upper-body exercise."

Ruth raised her arm and jiggled the flesh beneath her upper arm. "Sounds like a good idea. Sure. If you can get it in my garage, you can keep it there. Can I use it?"

Helma was silent and Ruth guffawed. "Just joking. I've never set foot in a canoe."

"Never? What about summer camp?"

"*You* went to summer camp, Helma. I sat home and brooded in my bedroom to spite my parents, remember? Although Wilson Jones and I once stole a johnboat and hid it downstream on Scoop River. It's probably still there."

The hard-packed trail rose out of the ravine and meandered between new stylishly pale apartment buildings and a small park. Sunspot Acres was just across the park, set back in trees that couldn't quite hide the squalid cabins and trailers. There'd been talk of "cleaning it out" for years but so far a foolproof legal way hadn't been found.

"I'm beginning to believe this place is as bad as they say," Ruth said as they exited the perimeter of the park and walked through the trees behind Sunspot Acres.

Helma surveyed the rubbish that had been discarded

behind the cabins: tires, a gutted stove, a child's shattered plastic slide, garbage bags, a mouldering couch, rusted bed springs. Television voices rose in the evening air, mixing a gunfight and a comedy. They rounded the last cabin to the rutted gravel parking lot of Sunspot Acres.

"Oh, this is our lucky day," Ruth said, pointing across the muddy parking area. "There's Radar himself."

"Radio," Helma corrected, studying the man tying a tarp over the loaded bed of a pickup truck. The outline of a chair filled one corner, a tall oblong another; the rest of the contents appeared to be boxes.

Helma judged Radio to be in his late fifties or early sixties. He was a big man, bulkier than tall, with a spider tattooed on his left forearm, and his gray hair tied in a ponytail by a red bandana. His nose was pushed lumpily to one side as if it had been broken long ago. Helma hung back, taking in the blue pickup, memorizing the license plate, eager to write it all in her notebook, under "Witnesses."

"Going somewhere?" Ruth asked.

He squinted at Ruth, lowering bushy gray eyebrows, showing no surprise, not even pausing as he tied down the tarp. "I thought you'd be in jail by now," he told Ruth.

"Sounds like you've been doing your best to put me there."

He finished the knot and patted the load. "Nope. Co-operating with the law, that's all."

"So that's why you're leaving town?"

"Just delivering items for a man."

Two toddlers stood in the doorway of one of the cabins, holding cans of pop and watching them. A plastic pot of purple petunias sat on the doorstep.

"Speaking of men," Ruth asked, "or people trying to be men, why was Lotz in jail?"

"He was framed," Radio told her. He leaned against his truck and picked at his front teeth with his thumbnail.

"For what?"

"Robbery."

"So why'd he come back here?"

Radio shrugged. "Nostalgia. This was home, I guess."

Helma noticed the way Radio's hair receded from his forehead, the familiar cheekbones, the thickened, arthritic knuckles. "You're Radio Lotz, aren't you?" she guessed. "Are you Joshman Lotz's brother?"

His look was so venomous Helma bit her lip but she continued to meet his dark eyes.

"My name's Kraft, and you're nosy."

"No, she isn't," Ruth disagreed. "But she *is* very perceptive. Was your brother living with you? Did you take him in when he got out of prison?"

"Get out of here. You," he said, pointing to Helma. "Drop that tarp."

"You have nice furniture for living in such squalid lodgings," Helma observed.

Radio clenched his fists and Helma casually stepped back beside Ruth.

"I should thank you for calling off your brother in Joker's but you were doing it for his sake, not mine," Ruth said. "I'll bet it was tough keeping him out of trouble, wasn't it? Did he mix you up in his little problems?"

"I said get out of here, you harpies."

"What happened after I left the bar? Was there another person interested in seeing Joshman Lotz dead? Or did you two continue your quarrel? Maybe you got really, really mad and accidentally killed him."

The red engorged look drained from Radio Kraft's face. His hands unclenched. He was suddenly calm as he took a single smooth step toward Ruth. The evening air around him pulsed with danger.

"Josh was going straight," he told Ruth, his voice low. "He'd paid his dues. He didn't owe anybody. You're forgetting I was in the bar. I was *there* and I heard you threaten Josh. I didn't leave the bar but *you* left and *he* left. And there he was, dead in *your* yard. Maybe you can dupe the cops into believing your story but I know better and I'll tell you one more thing." He leaned closer to Ruth. She stared at him, her mouth slightly open, frozen by his diatribe.

"If the cops don't get you for this, lady," he whispered, "I will."

Helma grabbed Ruth's arm and jerked her backward. Ruth stumbled and shook her head as if she'd been asleep.

"It's time to leave now," Helma said in her this-library-is-closing voice. "It's nearly dark."

Radio Kraft went back to straightening and smoothing his tarp. "Mind your little friend and get moving."

"I'm not little," Helma said, recognizing the immediate danger had passed but still not letting go of Ruth's arm.

"You are compared to the Purple People Eater here," he said, jerking a thumb at Ruth.

"You don't scare me," Ruth challenged. "You know I didn't kill your brother. You're just scared the police will believe *my* story." Her voice wavered. "And they will, too."

Radio Kraft walked casually from his pickup toward the cabins, his back to them.

"They *will*," Ruth called after him.

Helma continued pulling on Ruth until Ruth gave up and snapped, "Let go of me, Helma. He's lying. Why are you dragging me away?"

"This is the better part of valor. Take three deep breaths."

Ruth obediently gulped the night air like snores, putting her whole body into it.

"Now two more," Helma advised.

"I'm okay," Ruth protested, looking back at the cabin into which Radio Kraft had disappeared. "Do you think he meant it?"

"Which part?"

"The 'if the police don't get you I will' part."

Helma shook her head. "He's enraged over his brother's death. It's natural to blame someone else."

"Even when he's the killer?"

A dented and smoking white Pinto station wagon entered the Sunspot Acres parking lot and stopped, lurching twice.

"Hey, Miss Zukas!"

Ruth's face changed from agitated to speculative, eagerly eyeing the Pinto. "New friend of yours, Helma?"

"Library patron."

The man in the blue uniform got out of the battered Pinto, adjusted his belt, wiped at his shirt, smoothed back the sides of his hair, and sauntered over to Ruth and Helma, his shoulders swaying with each step. It was the library patron who called himself "Rock."

"Silence, my throbbing heart," Ruth murmured.

He pointed to the patch on his arm. Helma detected the lines of shoulder pads beneath the shirt's shoulders. "Security for You," the patch read, superimposed over a stylized smiley face. "You helped me get this baby," he said to Helma, his voice heartfelt with gratitude.

"The material was in the library," Helma told him. "It's what you did with it that counts."

"You're right," he quickly agreed.

"Do you live here?" Helma asked.

"For now. I'm looking at a real nice place. On the water."

"Do you know Radio Kraft?" Ruth asked, pointing toward Radio Kraft's pickup.

"The big guy with the tattoo? I know who he is. His brother got killed, everybody's saying."

"Were they living together?"

The security guard shrugged. "Couldn't say." He shifted his feet and waved toward the Pinto. "Had to drive my junker today. My car's in the shop."

"My other car is a BMW," Ruth said, reciting a line from a bumper sticker.

"How'd you know?" Rock asked seriously.

Now it was Ruth who pulled on Helma's arm. "We have to go," Ruth told Rock. "Bye."

"Want me to walk you home?"

"No, thanks."

As they reached Rose Trail, Ruth said, "Talk about dim bulbs. 'My other car's a BMW.' Hah."

"We're all . . ." Helma began.

"Don't give me old Sister Mary Martin's lecture about everybody being a different-sized receptacle for brains. We're talking thimbles and pea pods here."

The shadows deepened to almost complete darkness as the Rose Trail passed beneath the street. Spring peepers chorused on either side of the trail. Helma gasped at the bulk that suddenly moved in front of them.

"Sorry," a youthful voice said, accompanied by the sound of a zipper closing. "I was just taking a . . ."

"That's unsanitary," Helma informed the young man in her silver-dime voice. "There are restrooms not more than a hundred yards from here."

"Yes ma'am," the voice replied, already receding into the night.

Once clear of the trees, Helma stopped at a bench beneath a street light and sat down, removing her notebook from her purse. "I have to update my notes while the information's still fresh in my mind."

"He killed Lotz," Ruth said as Helma tried to write. "They were fighting in the bar when I showed up, I bet, and now he's trying to pin it on me. He thinks if he scares me good, I won't say any more to the police. He's wrong, though. He'll probably skip town. That's what's in his pickup: all his worldly possessions. He's planning to leave me twisting in the wind. God, Helm, what if he had the murder weapon and he's put it somewhere so it can be connected to me?"

"One moment, please, Ruth," Helma said as she swiftly filled a page and turned to the next. "I'm nearly finished."

Ruth strode back and forth across the path. "Do you *really* think they were brothers? Brothers don't kill each other, do they? I mean, I heard about Cain and Abel but do they do it in real life? Did you ever want to kill one of your brothers? We should have let that cop follow us to Sunspot Acres. They could have handcuffed the guy and dragged him off to jail, and given me back my life."

Helma returned her notebook to her purse and stood, smoothing down the front of her slacks. "It appears to me, with your quarrel with Lotz which was confirmed by several witnesses and since his body was discovered in your yard, the evidence leans more toward you than Radio Kraft."

"Helma!"

"Speaking strictly on the facts, Ruth. Not on my beliefs or intuition."

"What chance do I have if all we've got is your intuition?"

"Sooner or later, intuition will provide evidence."

" 'Sooner or later' could be cutting it close."

They returned through the back door of Joker's, quietly skirting the edge of the room while Kipper wiped the bar, and straight out the front door to Helma's car.

As she drove toward Ruth's house, careful to obey the speed limit, Helma glanced in her mirror, wondering about the car headlights behind her.

❧ chapter nine ❦

AIR FREIGHT

Patrice had been in Ms. Moon's office with the door closed for forty-five minutes. Ms. Moon espoused "open discussions" and "group sharing," so a conference behind closed doors was such a rare incident that all eyes were drawn to Ms. Moon's rainbow-decorated door as if it might suddenly dissolve to reveal the mysterious debate within.

Before closeting herself with Ms. Moon, Patrice had been grimly silent, failing even to respond to George Melville's unusual attempt to humor her by offering to fetch her a cup of coffee.

"What do you think's going on?" Eve asked Helma, frowning at the closed door and twisting a curl around her finger. "Do you think Patrice is in trouble because she won't chaperone an overnight camp-out?"

"I'm sure we'll be informed if we're meant to know."

"How can you be so disinterested?"

Helma wasn't disinterested. But at the moment library matters couldn't compete with the drama unfolding around Ruth and the murder of Joshman Lotz. Helma had known Ruth since they were both ten years old, nearly thirty years. Because of Ruth's art and their differing and frequently opposing habits, chunks of Ruth's life were outside of Helma's ken, but she *knew* Ruth.

It was true Ruth lied when it was convenient, was occasionally undependable, spoke too quickly and too loudly, and kept a disastrous house. But still, in situations that mattered, during *real* trouble, Ruth was as solid as . . . well, as Helma. Ruth's involvement in murder was simply inconceivable.

Patrice's extension rang. Four times, six times. Obviously the circulation staff was busy out front or they would have answered it by now. The electronic ring was as irritating as a car alarm. Helma was in no mood for additional irritation. She left her cubicle and answered Patrice's phone.

"This is Doctor Freeman's office, calling to remind you . . ."

"Patrice isn't in at the moment," Helma broke in. "May I take a message?"

"I'm calling to remind Patrice of her appointment."

Helma jotted the message components in all the proper spaces on a pink message pad and left it in the middle of Patrice's blotter. Dr. Freeman was Helma's doctor as well, one of the Bellehaven doctors sanctioned on the city's insurance plan. She saw Dr. Freeman annually whether she wanted to or not but rarely had reason to in between.

Helma's own phone buzzed. It was Mrs. Carmon at the circulation desk. "Miss Zukas, there's a man here to see you."

"Is it a salesman?"

"I don't think so. No. I'd definitely say not."

"Please ask who it is."

Mrs. Carmon came back on the line. "His name is Carter Houston."

"I'll be right there."

His back was to her but Helma easily recognized Detective Carter Houston by the shape of his body, the prim set of his feet. He stood in the reference section looking at a looseleaf *Facts on File* volume, giving Helma time to straighten her shoulders and prepare her professional smile.

"A kid could write a term paper out of one of these," Detective Houston said when he saw Helma, flipping pages and shaking his head.

"They frequently do. How may I help you?"

"Can we sit down a minute?"

"In the vestibule," Helma suggested.

The vestibule by the front doors, popular with children waiting for rides and teenage couples, was vacant. Helma and Detective Carter sat opposite one another on the institutional green Naugahyde chairs. The detective arranged the seams of his slacks and adjusted his tie before taking out his notebook. Helma removed hers from her skirt pocket and clicked open the ballpoint pen she'd inserted in the spiral binding. She flipped to a clean page under POLICE, jotted down the date, and wrote "Conversation with Det. C. Houston."

"Helma . . ." he began.

"Please call me Miss Zukas."

"Miss Zukas. You and Ruth Winthrop were seen at Joker's bar last night."

"And?"

"The bartender felt you were interested in Joshman Lotz."

"Wouldn't you be interested in someone you were accused of murdering?"

"Ruth Winthrop hasn't been accused of murdering anyone."

"Oh, then you must be here to discuss another matter?"

The detective regarded her, reminding her for a moment of the way Radio Kraft had glared at her. Again, she refused to look away or even to blink and Detective Houston's eyes veered away first, to his notebook and back, breaking their brief challenging encounter.

"You and your friend are taking this too lightly," he said, his jaws clenching, his lips tightening, his drawl more in evidence. "You're interfering in police matters, second-guessing our operations, and possibly even damaging our investigation."

"I never take death lightly," Helma assured the detective. "And I also never interfere with professionals who are adequately performing their jobs. Do you have something concrete you wish to ask or discuss with me?"

"To put it plainly, I'm asking you to mind your own business."

"I am," she said, closing her notebook and standing. "Now if you'll excuse me, I have work to do." She took a step away and then turned back, "You also might stay back a few more cars when you're doing surveillance. You're far too obvious to be effective."

Behind her, Detective Houston grunted but Helma continued from the vestibule without wavering or turning back.

At the bank of computer catalogs, Helma stepped up to the first empty terminal and typed in the name of the artist whose work Ruth had mentioned: Fernando Botero.

The library owned one book of his work. Helma retrieved it from the 750's in the oversized art shelves and sat on a stool at the back of the fiction stacks, away from the eyes of the public or the staff.

She nearly laughed aloud at the glossy page she randomly opened to: "The Poet," a depiction of a pudgy but dapper little moustached man reclining on a grassy hill. Ruth was right: Detective Carter Houston himself might have sat for Mr. Botero.

"Helma," Roberta said as Helma passed the reference desk. "Did you hear Patrice's news?"

"I'm not sure. What is it?"

"She's announced her retirement and this time she swears she means it."

Helma entered the workroom in time to hear Patrice say, "My younger sister's condominium is near Tucson. In a nice neighborhood. Separate from people on fixed incomes," she added.

"Naturally," George Melville commented.

"But your beautiful gardens," Eve said. "And Binky's grave."

Patrice nodded. "My single regret," she said with unusual candor. "The realtor has promised to look for an appreciative buyer, one who won't disturb . . . things."

"When will you be leaving?" Helma asked.

"July first. The beginning of the new fiscal year."

Helma detected the burgeoning wonder of unmasked excitement surrounding Patrice, a dreamy cast to her eye, the verge of a smile, an aura of new beginnings and unlimited possibilities.

George Melville counted off on his fingers. "That's about ten weeks to go through the hiring process for a new librarian. Not much time."

"I've volunteered to be a member of the search committee," Patrice said.

"Usually," Helma reminded her. "we're not involved in hiring our own replacements."

"It's like ruling from the grave," George said.

Patrice pursed her lips. "My position here is very specialized, requiring a highly trained, emotionally mature, and knowledgeable individual. Input from me will be invaluable."

Helma moved to the entrance to her own cubicle, feeling that yes, Patrice was recovering from her loss.

"Have you made a decision about the Snow to Surf Race yet?" Eve asked Helma.

"Eve told me," Patrice interrupted. "Participating in a canoe race is undignified for a serious librarian, I feel. It frivolitizes you in the eyes of the public."

"So you don't want to do it?" George asked Patrice sweetly. "Helma needs a partner."

"Certainly not," Patrice sniffed.

"I'll decide by Friday," Helma reminded them. "Please don't pressure me for a decision any sooner."

After George and Eve returned to their work stations, Helma stood and offered Patrice a chocolate from their gift box.

"I don't eat chocolate," Patrice said. "It gives me a headache."

"May I ask you a question, Patrice?"

"Is it library related?"

"No. It pertains to the man who was murdered: Joshman Lotz."

Patrice wrinkled her nose in distaste. "How curious you'd be interested in him. But go ahead."

"Did you see him after he was released from prison?"

"I wasn't aware he'd been incarcerated but the last time I saw him was fifteen, no: almost sixteen years ago. I remember because Binky was six months old and I was taking him to have his little operation and Cartier Street was blocked by an accident. Joshman Lotz was leaning against a car right in front of me while the police wrote him a ticket."

"You didn't like him."

Patrice firmly shook her head. "I didn't. Not many did, at least not nice people."

"What about his brother?"

"I believe it was a complicated family. There was a younger brother or two, and of course the one who became a doctor. 'The good one,' everybody called him."

"Doctor Robertson, the podiatrist?"

Patrice nodded. "But Joshman was the closest to me in age."

"You mentioned Joshman Lotz's infant son. Do you know what happened to him?"

"Not at all. I was living in San Francisco at the time. He was adopted out of the area, I understand."

"And it was a legal adoption?"

"As far as I know. There must be records somewhere." Patrice sighed. "Poor Alice. I'm glad she never knew what happened to her children."

"Children?" Helma asked. "There was more than one?"

"There was a girl. I don't remember her name but she was eight or nine when Alice died."

"Where is she now?"

"She's gone too. She drowned when she was a teenager. Out at Lake Wickersham, I believe. Or maybe Lake Pointer."

"Did he have other children, with his other wives?"

"I don't know. What did the obituary say?"

"It didn't mention any children at all."

"Then he probably didn't have any. Why are you interested in Joshman Lotz? You're not up to your amateur sleuthing again, are you, Helma?" Patrice asked, her upper lip rising.

"I was just curious."

Next, Helma visited Roberta's haphazard cubicle behind Eve's. Stacks of papers marked with yellow Post-It notes covered Roberta's desk.

Roberta had organized a troop from the Genealogy Club to laboriously index births and deaths in the *Bellehaven Daily News*, issue by issue, beginning with 1887. They were already up to the early seventies.

"Just put in the surname," Roberta told Helma. "The program provides a citation to the issue and page of the newspaper with the birth or death announcement. The club's next big project is to index arrests and convictions. You'd be surprised how often people request that information."

Helma sat at Roberta's computer and put in "Lotz." Twelve Lotz's appeared on the screen. There was Alice, dead at twenty-six. And earlier that same year: the birth of a son. Two more Lotzes in between, older. Then nine years after Alice Lotz's death: seventeen-year-old Catherine Lotz died. Helma printed out the list, tore it off the printer, then sat looking at it. What was the point? So Lotz had children. What did that have to do with Ruth's predicament?

But Helma rarely abandoned unfinished projects. She found the *Bellehaven Daily News* microfilm reel holding the year of young Catherine's death and reeled through it until she found the proper page. There she was. No picture. The headline read, "Teen Drowns in Tragedy." She'd swum out too far and went down before her friends could reach her. Divers had recovered her body and the funeral was scheduled in two days. Mother deceased. Father: Joshman Lotz.

Helma rewound the reel and turned off the microfilm reader. That had gained her nothing. Catherine Lotz, forever seventeen, would be forty-eight years old now if she'd lived.

"Phone call for you, Miss Zukas," Curt the page interrupted. "It's Ruth Winthrop. She says it's important."

Ruth thought all her calls were important. "Tell her I'll return her call this afternoon," Helma told Curt.

It was Helma's turn to take the lunch hour on the reference desk and she was surprised to see Chief Wayne Gallant approach the desk.

"I thought you had a noon meeting today," Helma blurted.

"I did but the judge's new secretary didn't know he has an inviolate bridge game every Tuesday noon. It's too bad you're working. I don't think either one of us was at our best at lunch yesterday. How about if we try it again and see if we come off any better?"

"I'm unsure what you mean, but if you were planning to question me, Detective Houston has already been here."

The chief grinned. "I'd be willing to bet he didn't get a shred of information from you."

"I had nothing to share with him," Helma said.

"That doesn't surprise me. Do you have anything to tell *me*?"

Helma shook her head.

"You have my number if you change your mind," he said. "Can I call you for a lunch date next week?"

"If it's convenient for you," Helma told him, wishing he'd stop smiling at her like that.

After her reference desk shift, Helma called the air freight office.

"Yeah, it's here," she was told. "Big sucker. Bring a truck."

"Can't you deliver it?"

"No can do. Gotta have somebody come get it."

Helma took two hours of comp time and left the library early. On her way home she stopped at the sports store and bought a life preserver and a canoe rack with protective pads.

"It's the best rack we've got."

"That's what I wanted."

"Easy to Attach!" the directions promised.

Easy for whom? Helma wondered as she struggled to attach the front bar to her car in the Bayside Arms parking ports.

"Oh, Faulkner," she said as she pinched her finger between the clamp and roof gutter.

"Can I give you a hand?" Walter David entered the parking area, carrying a red tool box. He wore khaki shorts and Helma raised her eyes from his very hairy and chubby legs.

"I have all the right tools," he said. He set down the tool box, nearly dropping it on his foot, then rolled his eyes upward. "I mean, to help you. For this job. You know."

"I'm fine. Thank you." Seeing his disappointment, she amended, "Perhaps if you could test it to make sure I have it on tightly enough."

"You bet. Did you buy a kayak?"

"My canoe is at the airport. I had it shipped from Michigan."

Walter David tightened the racks, then pulled on them, testing, rocking Helma's Buick. "Do you need any help picking it up?"

She politely declined and when she drove out of the Bayside Arms parking lot, Walter David stood watching her, holding his red tool box.

Helma paid the air freight charges with money from her "Effortless" account. Every night she dropped her change into a brown gallon jar her father had given her full of pennies when she was eight years old and which she suspected had once held whiskey. Each time it filled, she took the jar to the bank and deposited the money in a special account. It was her "effortless" money and everything she paid for with that money she considered to be free and guiltless, and often, secret.

Helma gave a ten-dollar bill to an eager teenager hanging around the air freight office to unpack her canoe. Bruce had packaged it in a handmade wooden crate, wrapped inside blue foam sheets for padding. The crate was scratched but her canoe was unscathed.

"Wow! This is cool," the teenager said as he respectfully unshrouded the glowing cedar canoe.

They were quickly surrounded by admirers who tentatively stroked the sleek wood, commented on the lines and craftsmanship. "That's a classic."

Helma hadn't seen her canoe in years. It *was* a "beauty," as one of the men proclaimed.

Uncle Tony had built it of northern white cedar strips with ash gunwales, decks, and thwarts. It had hand-caned seats and partially enclosed decks at the ends, a feature Uncle Tony had only added to the girls' canoes. "To store your lipstick," he'd teased them. The canoe was keelless, with V ends and a gently rounded bottom for speed, moderately rockered for maneuverability.

Helma walked around it, sliding a finger along the outer gunwale, admiring the curve of the tumblehome, picturing Uncle Tony in his garage, lovingly building his canoes with a passionate intensity the rest of the family indulged. Childless himself, he'd built a canoe for each of his nieces and nephews, bestowed shyly on twelfth birthdays, each one designed with that individual twelve-year-old in mind. Helma's was swifter and lighter and shorter than her cousin Ricky's, narrower beamed than Bruce's, longer than her cousin Susan's.

A styrofoam cooler was nestled beneath the center thwart, tied round with heavy twine. The teen lifted it out, sniffing. "Oh-oh, this smells kinda greasy," he said. "Like spoiled food or something. You sure you want it in your car? Want me to toss it?"

"Put it in the trunk with the paddles, please," Helma instructed him.

The blade of the bow paddle *was* warped as Bruce had warned, but Helma judged it repairable.

Helma wondered if in other circumstances or time, Uncle Tony would have been an artist like Bruce instead of a logger. Big, dreamy Uncle Tony, who, when she was in library school, had caught his heavy clothes climbing over a barbed wire fence while deer hunting, the gun discharging and Uncle Tony bleeding to death, found a frantic night later, snow-dusted, still caught on the barbs.

Without her asking, the men from the air freight office loaded the canoe on top of her Buick, lifting it reverently, cushioning it with extra foam sheets, fussing over its security. "Treat this baby good," one of the men advised her.

Helma was conscious of the glances as she drove through Bellehaven and at first she worried something dangerous was happening to her canoe but when she observed the faces more closely, she realized they wore expressions of admiration and covetousness.

Instead of going directly to Ruth's to store her canoe in Ruth's garage, Helma drove to the Bayside Arms, reluctant to part with her canoe so soon—and also to remove the cooler the teen had said smelled "greasy."

Inside her apartment, she undid the twine and opened the styrofoam box, removing potato *kugelis* and *suris*, the white cheese her grandmother used to make, bacon buns and sausages, inhaling deeply the scent of the Lithuanian foods of her youth. At the bottom of the box was a securely wrapped and taped plastic package. Helma carefully opened it, knowing from the smell what it contained before she slit the tape.

Smoked chubs. Three golden, greasy, eyes sunk in their sockets, smoked whitefish, laden with Lake Michigan pollutants. Grease wicked through all the layers of paper and still shone on their skins. They were disgustingly ugly, smelly, artery clogging, far too salty.

Helma peeled back the glistening golden skin of one of the chubs and picked off a piece of pale shiny flesh, setting it on her tongue. Boy Cat Zukas meowed and pawed the balcony door. Helma closed her mouth and sucked out the oils and salt and smoky flavoring before she swallowed.

Her phone rang when she'd nearly finished the first chub. She tore off a piece of paper towel and wrapped it around the receiver before she picked it up. It was Ruth.

"I'm sorry, Ruth," she hastily apologized. "I forgot to call you back. My canoe . . ."

"You can forget about storing it in my garage," Ruth said.

"It won't take much room."

"No. That's not it at all," Ruth said wearily. "My garage burned to the ground this morning and guess who thinks I did it to destroy evidence?"

❦ chapter ten ❦

BURNING QUESTIONS

Wisps of smoke still rose from Ruth's garage, which had caved in on itself in a shockingly small pile of rubble. Charred wood and broken glass, mysteriously twisted metal, the windowless black hulk of her Saab. The periwinkle that had edged the garage where Joshman Lotz's body had lain was burned away. The paint on the side of Ruth's house closest to the garage was blistered, her clematis plant leafless and dead, its trellis blackened.

Helma parked beside the fire department's barricade. The air was rank, blue tinged.

"It ain't a pretty sight, is it?" Ruth asked, standing on her sidewalk, leaning against a shovel. Her clothes were smoky and blackened as if she'd tried to fight the fire herself. An ashy smear circled her nose and mouth.

"What was the cause?"

"The suspicion at this point is arson, I guess. Wouldn't you know it started when there was nobody shadowing me. I was asleep when Rob Stone next door pounded on my door. It must have taken all of five minutes to burn up and collapse. Couldn't save a damn thing. Luckily, I never keep enough gas in my car, or it might have blown up the whole neighborhood. Poof." She stared at the smoking ruins. "Who'd have thought I'd grieve for a *car*, for pity's sake. But there it is. I'd like to shed a few tears and maybe have a cookie-and-tea memorial service like Patrice did for Binky."

"You said the police accused you of destroying evidence?"

Ruth idly twirled the shovel back and forth, closing her red eyes for a moment before she answered. "Not in those exact words, of course. Our crafty Detective Houston operates too much by the book to give away his treasured suspicions. It's his ... demeanor, you know. Pointed questions about what I kept in there: sharp garden tools, ropes and chains, racks and handcuffs, that sort of thing."

Ruth stepped forward and distractedly pushed back coals on the sidewalk that had spilled out of the foundation. "And *this* time, he *did* warn me not to leave town. Not that I have the means anymore." She turned to Helma with a wry smile. "I'm beginning to believe I'm in *real* trouble, Helm."

"Helma," Helma corrected, studying the ruin, thinking that in a way, it was like looking at a lifeless body. The past erased, the only evidence of existence now memories. Why burn Ruth's garage? Was it coincidence or *had* it contained damaging evidence and if so, damaging to *whom*?

"You gotta stick to me," Ruth said. "I'm not going anywhere without you."

"Why?"

"Not even newly ordained Detective Carter Houston could believe *you'd* be involved with a criminal."

"He's not overly fond of me, either."

"He doesn't have to be. He just has to know you're a paragon."

"But Ruth, *what* was in your garage someone might want to destroy?"

Ruth looked skyward. The sun had passed over the trees and the clouds to the west glowed while the sky overhead waned progressively duller, from dusty blue to textureless gray. The afternoon air was permeated with the odor of burnt wood and refuse, tinged with a smell like burnt chemicals.

"Some paintings that deserved to burn, gardening stuff I hardly ever used, a pretty nice aluminum extension ladder. And my car. That's about it."

"Could somebody have hidden the murder weapon inside?"

"Sure. I never locked it. Convenient, eh?"

"Too convenient."

"Maybe this is just a little love note from Radio Kraft," Ruth suggested. "My garage, my car. What's next?"

"Discuss it with the police," Helma urged her. "Call them."

"Or I can just wait until they make their daily visit."

"The fire appears extinguished," Helma said. "Have you been out here all day?"

Ruth nodded. "Since the fire truck left. On guard against loose sparks getting out or stray kids getting in. Twice already I've chased out the little thugs who live across the alley." She looked down at her dirty and smoky clothes. "I *look* like a fire bug, don't I? Guess I should change clothes. Want to come in?"

Helma shook her head. "Will you be all right? Do you want to stay at my apartment?"

"You mean as the dead of night approaches and visions of flames dance in my head?" She shivered in exaggerated horror. "I'm okay. I wouldn't feel right leaving this mess."

"At least lock your door and secure your windows."

"Will do." Ruth glanced into the alley at the silhouette of Helma's Buick and the canoe on its roof. She whistled, leaned her shovel against the house and walked around Helma's car, smoothing her hand over the cedar hull that gleamed even in the darkening evening.

"God, Helma. This is gorgeous! Why didn't I realize that twenty years ago? You can't take a work of art like this down a *river*. You'll destroy it. Borrow somebody else's canoe. I'll even pitch in so you can rent a nice high-tech job."

Helma shook her head. "I know this canoe. It's the only one I'd feel confident paddling—if I decide to participate in the race, that is."

"So now that my garage is no longer an option, where are you going to keep it? Can you rent a storage unit?"

Helma tugged at the ropes holding the canoe, testing the knots, reluctant to store it anywhere out of her sight, wondering wildly for a moment whether it would fit in her living room, parallel to her coffee table and bookcases.

"I'll leave it on my car until I find a suitable place," she told Ruth.

Ruth stepped back and framed Helma and her Buick and canoe in her hands as if she were snapping a photo. "This will be a sight to behold: Miss Wilhelmina Zukas driving around Bellehaven with a canoe strapped to the roof of her twenty-one-year-old Buick."

"I see cars carrying canoes in Bellehaven every day. It's nothing unusual."

"We're talking Helma Zukas here."

"What are you implying, Ruth?"

"Never mind."

"I'm going home, then."

"I'll be here playing fireman, guarding against that volatile lurking ember."

Helma slept lightly, wakened by the slightest sound outside the Bayside Arms: passing traffic, a boat's horn, a barking dog. Several times during the night she rose from her bed and parted the curtains in her back bedroom to peer out at the carports. Each time, when she detected the dark end of her canoe extending beyond her car, still there, untouched, she sighed and returned to bed.

When her clock radio turned on, Helma was exhausted, her eyes scratchy and puffed, her head aching. She groggily reached one arm from beneath the covers and turned off the radio. Then, unlike her, she drifted off to sleep again, dreaming of fires that burned prettily but did not consume.

A door banged somewhere and Helma sat upright, staring in shock at her digital clock. 8:10. She was already late for work, late for the second time in less than a week.

Instead of jumping from her bed and rushing to the shower, Helma sat on the edge of her bed with both feet flat on the floor, cleared her throat, patted her hair, and straightened her nightgown. She reached for her bedside phone and dialed the library's number.

"I'm feeling unwell and have decided to take a day's sick leave," she told Ms. Moon.

"I've never known you to be ill, Helma," Ms. Moon said in a voice rich with concern. "Whenever I feel ill, it helps me to meditate on my body's needs. Have you tried that?"

"I haven't risen yet," Helma told her.

"Take as much time as you need to regain your natural rhythms. We can cope here."

Helma hung up, closing her eyes for a long moment, wondering why even a brief conversation with Ms. Moon left her yearning for a nap.

It was the first aimless day off Helma could remember. Shapeless, no appointments to keep or errands to run. She considered lounging in bed for another hour or so and actually went so far as to lay her head back on her pillow and pull her blankets to her chin.

But after five minutes of gazing with wide-open eyes at the white ceiling fixture, wondering if that was a natural flaw in the glass or a dead fly, she was up and heading for the shower.

The day was fair, calm and partly sunny. Buttering her toast, Helma glanced out at the blue waters of the bay, thinking what a good day it was for boating, when she remembered her canoe. She *could* be out on the water. Not the bay; it was too unpredictable for her little craft.

Helma's joy in open water came from the visual experience, from viewing the ocean or the Great Lakes from shore or the railings of very large vessels. When she was aboard a smaller boat, she preferred rivers and lakes where the banks and shorelines were clearly visible, offering boundaries and safe haven.

Helma's skills were too rusty to launch her canoe into a river. She swallowed her last bite of toast and sipped her orange juice, pondering the lakes close to Bellehaven.

Lake Wickersham, the lake on the eastern edge of Bellehaven where Catherine Lotz had drowned, was too large, too deep. Carved out by glaciers, it stretched for miles between forested hills, with uncertain winds sweeping unexpectedly out of the foothills.

Lake Pointer would do. A small lake protected by dense trees. Nearly always calm. Not too far to swim to shore from any point if it became necessary. Although in all her years of canoeing, Helma had only rolled her canoe once, and that hadn't been her fault; it had been her cousin Ricky's.

She shook her head, banishing the image of Ricky's face before it could fully form, and began a mental list of items to take to the lake with her. After finding the system for a patron, Helma had taken to patterning her own mental lists after the ancient Greek *lochi* system of arranging items on parts of her body, beginning with her head. Most important was a life vest; she imagined it hanging over the top of her head; she mentally hung her hat on her left ear, pictured sunscreen sticking out of her right ear and a bottle of water balanced on the end of her nose. The more ridiculous the image the better; it never failed.

"Too much work," Ruth had proclaimed when Helma had explained her new system. "Why not just make a list?"

"Because you don't always have pencil and paper."

"If you can't get to a pencil and paper it's not worth remembering."

Barbra Streisand finished singing, "The Way We Were" on the radio, followed by the local news. Helma leaned forward and turned up the volume.

"A drug bust last night at Sam and Ella's, a local restaurant, netted five hundred thousand dollars worth of cocaine, Chief of Police Wayne Gallant said at a news conference early this morning."

Sam and Ella's, where she and Chief Gallant had eaten lunch. Helma smiled, wondering if Wayne Gallant harbored any new opinions of her "observant" nature.

A light mist still hung along the shadier shores of Lake Pointer when Helma backed her car close to the boat ramp and got out. No other boats were on the lake yet. The deep calm water near shore mirrored the tall trees, lightening in the center to the blue and white reflection of the sky. No motors were allowed on Lake Pointer and it was a peaceful place.

Helma shielded her eyes and peered across the lake, where a bald eagle occupied a solitary snag. Either it or its relatives had frequently sat there for years, a dark shape brooding over the forest and water. One spring Helma had seen it swoop majestically down on a family of ducks and carry away a futilely quacking duckling that had lagged at the end of the line of siblings.

Helma undid the cross tiedowns and hitchknots that held her canoe. Then she positioned herself beside her Buick and without thinking about it so she wouldn't confuse herself, she slid the bow end off her car roof and slipped beneath the yoke. Her canoe only weighed fifty-one pounds and after all these years it was an easier carry than she expected.

On the little dock beside the boat ramp, Helma rolled the canoe onto her knee and slipped it into the water where it floated high, light, and so beautiful she wished she'd brought her camera. She tied the lines to the dock cleats and donned her life preserver. Then she leaned down, placed one foot in the center of the canoe, a hand on each gunwale, and lightly stepped aboard, barely rocking the little craft.

Her canoe could carry two people; Uncle Tony had hand-caned two canoe seats, but when it held two, it settled into the water, slow, an overweighted race horse, a bird with clipped wings, ordinary. When she was alone, as she usually had been, she knelt stern forward with her hips against the bow seat, the edges of which Uncle Tony had broadened and smoothed for just that reason. But after seventeen years, Helma sat stern forward, on the seat, at least to begin with.

Helma cautiously pushed away from the dock, aware of every hiss and bubble of water, the instability of her balance. She kept close to the shore, leaning a little into the right side of the canoe, ending each forward stroke in a slight swoop to keep the canoe on a straight course.

"The power's in your upper hand," Uncle Tony had instructed. "Completely relax between each stroke. You'll paddle forever without wearing down."

Helma listened to Uncle Tony's voice over the water, whispering along the sides of her canoe.

"Feather your blade more, Billie. You're working against yourself. Draw in more at the beginning. Good, good. Twist your body, not your arms. Now you're remembering. Now you've got it. Good girl."

Once she winced when the paddle thwunked! against the wooden skin, seeing before her Uncle Tony's pained face.

The canoe drew only a few inches of water and responded to her slightest movement as she continually corrected herself, relaxing, coordinating her breathing and paddle strokes until her course was smooth and steady.

She pivoted, first one direction, then the other, daring each time to turn a little tighter, to reach out farther in her brace.

"Beautiful canoe!" a woman running the shore in a pink jogging suit called to Helma. Helma waved and took the opportunity to drift, stretching her back and shoulders, flexing her hands. Her body didn't know these movements any longer.

She slipped from the seat to kneel on a cushion, heeling her canoe even farther, her legs braced. In a scallop of water among close alder trees, she cautiously stood, concentrating on her trembling legs, knowing a wrong move would shoot her canoe from beneath her.

Finally, Helma knelt and did her favorite stroke, the Indian stroke, although she supposed by now it was called something more politically correct than the name they'd given it as children.

Never taking her paddle from the water, rotating the grip in the palm of her hand on the return. A silent, stealthy stroke that made her swift movements across the water noiseless.

The sun warmed her. A trout jumped off her port side. A joyful contentment settled over Helma as she crossed, recrossed, and edged Lake Pointer. On Scoop River, she'd sometimes drifted for a mile or more, letting the current pull her, dipping her paddle now and then to avoid logs or keep her transit straight. Lakes were pleasant but rivers . . . oh, the movement of rivers was truly a joy.

Three elderly men stood watching as Helma paddled up to the dock. Her shoulders and elbows burned; the small of her back felt as if it had been punched. Helma knew she wasn't in condition for a river, but with more training the canoe leg of the Snow to Surf Race was a definite plausibility.

"What a beauty," one of the men said, motioning to Helma's canoe. "Somebody build it for you?"

"My uncle."

"Does he still make them?" a bald man asked as he leaned down and held the bow for her. When she stood her stomach growled; it was long past lunch time.

"He died several years ago."

"That's a shame. Can we help you get it on your car?"

"I'd be very grateful," Helma said, stretching her shoulders and feeling very grateful indeed.

The three men spent undue time arranging the canoe on the Buick's carrier, checking the lines and examining the sleek wood, muttering together about how there just wasn't any fine craftsmanship anymore and the world was going to hell on a handtruck.

Helma drove home by way of Ruth's house, parking behind the burned garage. Ruth's Saab shell had been towed away but the burnt odor lingered. Acrid and unsettling. A note was tacked to Ruth's door saying, "Ken—I got tired of waiting so I'm already at Tanya's. See you there."

So much for keeping a low profile. Helma walked around the burned garage, intently eyeing the ruins but avoiding stepping close enough to dirty her shoes, wondering what could have been inside that was so damaging someone had burned the entire garage to keep anyone else from discovering it.

Ruth's shovel still leaned against the side of the house. Helma considered the shovel, then Ruth's freshly dug garden. Spring awakened Ruth. Each year she dug around in the dirt, preparing the way for a garden she rarely planted and if she did, always neglected and finally mowed over.

Helma retrieved the warped canoe paddle from her car, then with the shovel, wincing as she lifted the first shovelful, dug a shallow hole in the damp earth. The dirt around Bayside Arms was too rocky. She laid the paddle in the depression and covered it over, patting the dirt solid. She'd check it in a week. That should do it.

"Mother," Helma said casually over the phone. "Has anyone in your apartment building mentioned the man who was murdered last week? It seems like someone there might have known him."

"N.O.K.D.," Helma's mother replied. It was a term she'd adopted from a British TV show. Not our kind, dear, it meant. "But," she went on. "Jenny Allen on the third floor, the one whose daughter married the Honda dealer? She said years ago the dead man tried to sell her husband a stolen boat."

"How did he know it was stolen?" Helma asked.

Lillian laughed delightedly. "Because it was her brother-in-law's boat!"

As they spoke, Helma fanned the pages of the library book on the table in front of her. It was titled *Complete Canoeing Techniques*. Helma had abandoned it after the second chapter. She supposed she'd naively learned as a child the same techniques that were illustrated in the book, but reading about paddling in relation to the physics of wind, water, and physical force left Helma bored and distant.

Helma's mother cleared her throat. "Are you helping Chief Gallant again, dear?" she asked.

"The chief has a very competent staff," Helma assured her mother.

"Oh, but a man benefits from a woman's point of view, I always say."

Peter Robertson was the only podiatrist listed under Physicians in the yellow pages. When Helma dialed his office number, he answered the phone himself, catching Helma unprepared.

"I expected a receptionist," she said.

"She stepped out," Doctor Robertson said. "Can I help you?"

Helma had intended to make an appointment, but now she said, "This is Helma Zukas. I'm requesting information about your brother."

There was silence, then Doctor Robertson tersely said, "I don't have a brother."

"Joshman Lotz?"

"He's dead."

"I know. Can you . . ."

"I have no interest in discussing Joshman Lotz."

"What about Radio Kraft?"

"He may as well be dead. Now excuse me." And the telephone clicked in Helma's ear.

Helma's doorbell rang just after dark. She was sitting gingerly in her rocking chair, nursing her sore shoulders.

Her copy of the *Home Medical Guide* recommended ice packs for overused muscles. Lacking ice packs, Helma balanced a plastic bag of frozen peas on her left shoulder and corn on her right. A dessert plate holding a half-eaten slice of *kugelis* sat on her coffee table. She didn't move, waiting for whoever was at her door to leave. They rang twice more, then just when she thought they were gone, rang again.

She gave up, returned the corn and peas to her freezer and the *kugelis* to her refrigerator, then looked through the peep hole in her door.

It was Walter David. Now what? Reluctantly she opened the door.

Walter David was excited. He raised and lowered his eyebrows. He shifted from foot to foot, his face bright in the light from her kitchen.

"I just got home and caught some guy messing with your canoe," he said breathlessly. "I scared him off."

Helma pushed past him to the railing that faced the parking area. "Did he damage it?"

"I don't think so. He cut one of the ropes. Bet you anything he was trying to swipe it."

Helma raced down the steps, with Walter David heavily puffing behind her. "Did you get a good look at him?"

"No. Sorry. I just saw he was a big guy."

"You couldn't see if he had long hair or tattoos?"

Walter David shook his head. "Sorry," he apologized again.

Helma's canoe appeared untouched. The line tied to the rear bumper dangled free and the canoe was bumped to the edge of the carrier. Helma circled the canoe, running her hands along its sleek sides, Walter David at her heels, still puffing.

"I was thinking," Walter David said from behind her. "Apartment 1C is empty. You know, where Mr. Swayze died, I mean, lived. If you want, we could put your canoe in there. The painters can't get to it for a couple weeks. I can give you a key."

Helma was touched. "Are you sure it would be all right with the owner?"

"He's in California. He'll never know."

"That's very kind of you."

Helma at the bow end and Walter David at the stern, they carried Helma's canoe across the parking lot and into 1C, setting it wall to wall in the middle of the stale-smelling living room, where Mr. Swayze had spent his last days surrounded by medicine, oxygen, and a TV that was kept on too loud twenty-four hours a day.

🦎 chapter eleven 🦎

CANOE TACTICS

"**I**'m pleased to announce that Miss Helma Zukas has ended the suspense and graciously agreed to compete in the canoe leg of the Snow to Surf Race," George Melville announced to the little group in the staff lounge.

"Fantastic!" "Good going!" "All right!" Helma heard among the enthusiastic applause. Six team members and George Melville, the self-appointed team coach, crowded the little lounge, all of them the requisite library employees the local government division demanded, both professional and nonprofessional. The room pulsed with enthusiasm, high good health, and athletic prowess.

"So now," George continued. "We are a completely official relay team. And here's our illustrious lineup: Junie will lead the pack at the ski area with the four-mile cross-country skiing leg and hand off to Eve who downhill skis two and a half miles to slip the wristband to Tommy who runs eight miles down the mountain, handing off to Jeff who then bicycles like a madman for thirty-six miles. And then," here George Melville nodded to Helma, "Helma takes the wristband and launches her canoe from heaven, to paddle eighteen miles down the Nitcum to Roger who's waiting to slog his mountain bike nine miles through muddy trails and over fields to Weber who kayaks five miles across the bay."

George stopped his recitation and took a loud, chest-heaving inhalation. "And that, my dear friends, takes us triumphantly eighty-five miles and four thousand vertical feet to the finish line."

"Ta-da!" Weber, the bookmobile driver and kayaker cried, clasping his hands above his head.

"I *am* curious," Helma commented. "Which of you has been on a Snow to Surf team before?"

Feet shifted, eyes veered away from Helma's.

"I've watched," Jeffrey said.

"Yeah, me too."

"So have I."

"Then I gather none of us has lost our initial enthusiasm," Helma said, thinking that one experience in this race might be sufficient for a lifetime.

"Who's your partner?" Roger the mountain bicyclist asked Helma. Helma thought of Roger's direct competition on the planning department's team, his own ex-wife, wondering if Roger knew.

"I intend to perform as a solo canoeist," Helma told him.

Roger turned to George, his eyebrows raised.

"I checked," George said. "It's unusual but there aren't any rules against it."

More glances were exchanged between team members. "Miss Zukas," Jeffrey, the heavily freckled bicyclist and circulation page, said hesitantly, rising from his perch on the counter. "This means you'll have to take the hand-off from me, the biker, run down to the banks of the Nitcum, and launch your canoe all by yourself. That's burning a lot of energy before you even hit the water."

"I'm aware of that and I don't anticipate a problem as long as we all practice our segments of the race adequately. I have no concerns about my ability."

Jeffrey opened his mouth and raised his hand but then sat on the counter again and crossed his arms.

"I've ordered the t-shirts," Eve said. She nodded apologetically at Helma. "Sorry you joined too late to give your opinion. Here's a prototype." Eve held up a bright red t-shirt. On the front was a silk-screened open book and on the back, in large black letters, it read, "I'd Rather Be Reading."

"I don't normally wear that shade of red," Helma said.

"Wash it with a pair of new jeans," Roger offered. "That's what my ex-wife used to do all the time—dulls everything up real nice."

"Continue—or begin—individual training on your particular leg of the race," George told them. "We'll practice hand-offs Sunday after next. Roberta's in charge of the party at the race's end."

"Is that all?" Helma asked. "Don't we have any meetings with other teams or team officials?"

"What for?" George asked.

"To discuss the rules and strategies of the race."

"All I know is you start at the beginning and go as fast as you can to the end."

Helma picked up her yellow pad. The only words written on the page were, "Red t-shirts."

"I just bought this great one-piece ski outfit," Eve, the downhill skier, was telling Junie, the cataloging clerk and cross-country skier. "I hope the t-shirt won't make me look stupid."

"We don't have to win," Roger was saying to no one in particular, "but I'd like to see us beat the pants off the planning department.

"Helma," Ms. Moon called from her office door as Helma left the lounge. Ms. Moon waved a sheet of paper, smiling. "I have your memo. Of course you may leave early to practice canoeing. The library's indebted to you for saving the Snow to Surf team."

"However," Helma pointed out, "this *does* mean I won't be able to chaperone the children's overnight on May twenty-eighth."

Posters promoting Ms. Moon's library camp-out program were appearing all over town. Cute kids camped on an open book toasting marshmallows over a fire that threatened to engulf *Little Women*.

Ms. Moon pouted prettily. "That's a disappointment, isn't it? But as I promised, I'll take your place and maybe the next session of Camp-Out in a Book will be a happier one for you."

"I'm not sure it could be."

"You're not going to believe this," Ruth said into Helma's ear.

Helma glanced around the workroom. Patrice sat idly at her desk, not even bothering to hide that she was working a crossword puzzle. George Melville and Roberta stood close together behind piled boxes of newly arrived books. Through Ms. Moon's open door came the dulcet tones of Ms. Moon on the phone. Helma hesitated to ask Ruth what she wasn't going to believe. Another murder? More fire? A brush with Detective Carter Houston or Radio Kraft?

"I'm hot property," Ruth announced in a giddy voice.

"What do you mean?"

"Word's out that I'm a murder suspect and my stock is definitely on the rise. You know Wally at the gallery? He called a few minutes ago wanting more of my stuff. Every painting he had sold in the last couple of days."

"Because you're a murder suspect?"

"Yep. Ain't it grand? He wants to price the next batch higher."

"But Ruth, it's due to your notoriety, not your artistic skill."

"As they say: there's no such thing as bad publicity. Just think what'll happen if I become an *official* suspect; I could cut up my paint-gunked t-shirts, frame 'em, and make a fortune."

"I stopped by late yesterday afternoon, but you weren't home. You said you'd only leave your house in my company until the police arrested the real killer."

"I got bored, a little stir crazy, you know, so I went to

this sort of barbecue," Ruth said. "No harm done. So how does your little boat go?"

"The canoe's fine but I'm a little rusty. I'm taking it out again right after work."

"Can I come with you? I can't stand staying home."

"It's not very exciting, Ruth."

"Please. I'll stay home and paint diligently all day and be ready for a break. Okay?"

"If you stop by the Sports Corral and rent a life preserver."

"I don't need one."

"Ruth I *know* you can't swim."

"Well, I *know* you're not going to dump me in the drink."

"No one rides in my canoe without a life preserver."

"Aye-aye, Captain Bligh," Ruth said grumpily.

Ms. Moon had just pushed colored pins into a blue notice on the staff bulletin board. Helma stopped to read it.

"Annual Self-Defense Refresher Course!"

Helma inwardly groaned. The announcement was couched in terms of enthusiastic enticement, but Helma knew better. Attendance was mandatory. All city employees, men and women, young and old, able-bodied or not, had to present themselves in the city prison gym at their allotted times, where they learned defensive maneuvers and coping tactics. Since they all learned the same skills, Helma had often wondered who would have the advantage if a city employee decided to attack a city employee.

Coincidentally, Walter David was measuring walls for paint in 1C when Helma arrived to retrieve her canoe, causing him to pocket his silver retractable tape measure and hoist the bow end, despite Helma's protestations that she could do it herself.

"My pleasure, my pleasure," he said as he tied an efficient half hitch knot in the new rope. "Are you taking her down the river?"

There it was again, that curious habit of men to label

everything they rode—cars, boats, planes—as feminine.

"No. Just to Lake Pointer."

"That's a nice lake," Walter David said.

"Yes. I know it is."

"Real nice. I enjoy Lake Pointer, but I don't get much of a chance to go out on it because I don't own a boat."

"They're definitely worth saving for," Helma told him. "Have a pleasant evening."

"I've got a present for you," Ruth said when she'd closed the passenger door. "They're for the race." She handed Helma a box the length of a shoe box but wider, the lid and bottom wrapped separately in plain brown paper decorated with dashes and dots of violet paint.

"For the race?" Helma repeated.

"Yeah, I *know* you don't have any like this."

"Thank you," Helma said, setting the box on the seat between them.

"Aren't you going to open it?"

"I thought you said it was for the race."

"Would you just open it, puh-lease. It's a *gift*."

With both hands, Helma lifted off the lid. Ruth leaned toward her, smiling widely in anticipation, like a child who couldn't stop herself from blowing out her friend's birthday candles.

Helma pulled aside the tissue paper.

"So what do you think? Do you love 'em?"

Nestled together in the box, sole to sole, was a pair of fire-engine red, canvas high-top sneakers, the kind Helma had noticed middle-school boys wearing, sometimes girls, sometimes college students who affected torn jeans and flannel shirts, but not almost-thirty-nine-year-old librarians who didn't own any type of sneaker at all.

"You see," Ruth went on. "They're perfect for the race. You can run in them; it's okay to get them wet, and best of all, they give you ankle support—vital when you're scrambling across rocks to get to your canoe. The canoe guy at the Sports Corral recommended high-tops."

"They're red," Helma said, still not touching the sneakers.

"No kidding, Sherlock. They'll match your team shirt."

"They're *very* red."

"So exchange them for a different color." Ruth picked up the two red sneakers and set them side by side on the dashboard. They appeared very large, very tall. "Don't you like them?"

"That's very thoughtful of you, Ruth. Thank you. Really." Helma touched one finger to the striped laces. "Would you mind if I exchanged them?"

"Go ahead. Maybe the red *is* a little bright."

Helma returned the shoes to their box and covered them. It was more than just the color she intended to exchange.

Ruth's life jacket was—not surprisingly—bright purple with a pink zigzag stripe across the back.

"The guy at the Sports Corral called it a P.F.D.," Ruth said.

"It means personal floatation device."

"Well, I thought he said it was a B.F.D. and I told him I agreed."

After they set the canoe in the water, Ruth stood on the dock and dropped her life jacket in the bottom of the boat.

Helma knelt down, retrieved it, and handed it back to Ruth. "They work best when they're worn."

"Nobody actually *wears* one of these things, Helm. Well, except for you. Don't be such a stickler."

"If you wait until a life jacket is *necessary*, when there's a desperate emergency and you truly need one, it's too late to get it on."

"It's never too late to get it on," Ruth said, laughing for no reason.

"Ruth," Helma said firmly. "If you're riding in my canoe, you'll wear a life vest."

"You didn't say on the phone that I had to *wear* it, only *bring* it."

Helma turned her back to Ruth and knelt on the dock as if she were about to board her canoe and launch off alone into the calm blue waters of Lake Pointer.

"All right, all right. Calm down, damn it. Just wait 'til I zip this frigging straitjacket."

Helma struggled to hold her canoe steady as Ruth awkwardly climbed into it, rocking it precariously before she sat down on the bow seat facing Helma.

"You might want to sit the other way around," Helma suggested.

"I'm in. I'm not moving. You've only got one paddle anyway."

The canoe was sluggish, overburdened, but Helma considered it good exercise for her paddling muscles, which still ached from the previous day's excursion. With the added weight, she continually switched the paddle from side to side.

She may as well have been paddling a different boat. The other canoe, her real canoe, only existed when Helma paddled alone.

"Should this boat be this tippy?" Ruth asked.

"Just sit still and it'll be fine."

"If you say so. Do you think there are official cops' eyes peering at us through the branches?" Ruth asked, waving a hand toward the treed shores of Lake Pointer.

"I wouldn't be surprised."

Ruth sat straighter, tugging down the front of her life vest. "I wonder if I should have called them last night."

"Why?" Helma asked. "What happened?"

"Nothing, really, but that guy scares the hell out of me."

"Ruth. What guy?"

"Radio Kraft."

"Did you see him? What did he say?"

"He didn't say anything. Last night? I walked over to Tanya's. It's only about a mile and I knew Ken would bring me home, so I was almost to her house and there was our friend, Mr. Kraft, sitting in his pickup, pulled into a driveway. I had to walk right past him." Ruth shuddered. "He shot me with about a thousand invisible bullets. I was so scared I nearly screamed out Carter Houston's name. I knew he had to be around somewhere." Ruth gripped both gunwales and straightened her legs, gasping when the canoe rocked.

"Did you see Radio Kraft after that?"

"Not really."

Helma made two strong sweeping strokes on her right, pulling hard, and the canoe began turning back toward shore, tipping a little.

"Okay, okay. Cut it out," Ruth said. "I kept getting hang up calls last night after Ken brought me home. Nobody there. About every forty-five minutes."

"Did you press star 57?"

"What's star 57?"

"A way to trace calls. Do you think it was Radio Kraft?"

"Unless it was Detective Houston, checking in by phone. Who else would it be?"

"I don't know. Have the police talked to you again?"

Ruth shook her head. "Maybe when we get back to land, dear pucker-face Detective Houston'll be waiting with the cuffs and it'll be bye-bye, Ruthie."

"You haven't done anything, Ruth, and the police don't arrest people on a whim."

"That's what you say. Radio Kraft is the one who offed his brother, I could smell it on him. Did you catch that look on his face when I accused him? Guilt written all over it. Why is he pretending I did it? I'd like to quiz that guy under bright lights."

"*You* can't go near Radio Kraft again."

"Yeah, yeah. I know. And I don't want him near me, either. But what are the police waiting for? Why haven't they picked him up?"

"They can't make an arrest without evidence."

"Mmm." Ruth pointed toward shore. "Look at that guy in the trees fishing. Isn't he out of season?"

"I'd say so."

"Do you think anybody went to Lotz's funeral? We

should have gone just so we could see. I'll bet Radio Kraft didn't even show."

"He was Lotz's closest relative as far as I could tell, except for an estranged brother. His daughter's dead, his son's adopted."

"Sorta 'Ozymandias'-ish." Ruth said.

A few people were visible in the park that edged Lake Pointer. Others walked or jogged the shady trail, which Helma sometimes walked, that circumnavigated the lake. It took her forty-three minutes, forty-five when she stopped to look up at the bald eagle.

A lone man in a rowboat drifted in the center of the lake. It was tranquil, soft-aired. A swallow skimmed the water's surface, barely ruffling it, swooping after insects. The lake, the slanty sun, water riffling along the paddle's edge, the gentle movement, began to work its charms.

"This is nice." Ruth trailed her fingers through the water. "Wish I knew somebody with a *big* boat, like a yacht." She sighed. "Unfortunately, the men *I* hang out with can barely afford their paints and modeling clay."

"What about Paul?"

Ruth's face softened. "Yeah, but Minneapolis is too, too far away. He's not my type, anyway. Too quiet, too conventional, too . . . boring. And a frozen-foods middle management executive? That's crazy. We have absolutely nothing in common."

Helma lazily listened as Ruth continued arguing with herself over Paul, who Ruth couldn't seem to mentally discard as easily as she had other men in her life. There were more letters and late-night calls between Minneapolis and Bellehaven than Ruth let on, and aside from her two-week acquaintance with Paul a year and a half ago when he'd studied flash-frozen fish methods in Bellehaven, Ruth had made at least two known "stops" in Minneapolis on visits east, and Helma knew that some of Ruth's other trips and disappearances included rendezvous with Paul, too.

"So what about Chief Gallant?" Ruth suddenly asked, breaking into Helma's reverie.

Helma didn't miss a stroke. "He's investigating the murder to the best of his staff's ability."

"That's not what I'm talking about. I mean you and him." Ruth crossed her fingers. "You know, together. Any progress?"

It was the spell of the lazy day. "Not really. We see each other, but . . ."

Ruth nodded knowingly. "It's his divorce. I heard it was vicious. He's been burned and you're cautious. What a couple of . . . Good Lord! What's that?"

A buzzing whine, the water ten feet behind the stern spitting upward and almost simultaneously a crack! that echoed over the lake, its direction undetectable.

"Don't move," Helma warned, holding her paddle still, scanning the shadowed trees.

"What was it? It was a gun, wasn't it? I know it was a gun. Somebody's shooting at us, aren't they? Aren't they?"

Ruth, in her excitement, twisted from one side to the other, tilting the canoe. Helma pried her paddle in the rippled water, away from the side, turning the canoe in an agonizingly slow ninety-degree angle toward the nearest shore, struggling against Ruth's precarious, shifting weight in the bow. Water splashed onto her legs, the canoe yawed.

Another whine and a splinter of wood flew off the port gunwale between Helma and Ruth.

"Oh Geez Louise. Can't you go any faster? We're going to get killed." Ruth leaned over, reached into the water and paddled with cupped hands, throwing water in an arcing spray.

"Don't, Ruth!" Helma cried.

But it was too late. The canoe, assaulted beyond endurance, quietly and swiftly rolled over. For a brief moment, as the water closed over her head, Helma savored the tranquility beneath the surface, blurring and shimmering like magical liquid air, sounds soft and distant and benign. Movement became ballet-like, safe, not dangerous in the least.

Then, as Helma's life vest buoyed her to the surface, the cold water knifed through her. She bobbed above the water, fighting to fill her shocked lungs, and still holding her paddle, grabbed for her capsized canoe, aware of Ruth coughing and splashing in panic behind her.

"I'm going to die!" Ruth shouted.

Helma placed her paddle on top of her canoe bottom and, still holding securely to her canoe, she stroked toward Ruth, reaching for the shoulder of her bright purple life vest.

"No, you're not. Hold onto the canoe. Stay down."

Ruth spluttered but frantically clutched at the wooden canoe, pulling herself upward, out of the water.

"Don't," Helma ordered. "Get back in the water."

"Hell, no. This water is *ice*."

With all her strength, Helma jerked Ruth back off the canoe. "Are you trying to make yourself an easy target?"

"Oh," Ruth said, dropping beside Helma, letting her life vest hold her so only her head was out of the water. Her eyes bulged wide and her teeth chattered. "Is this like hiding behind the dead cavalry horse?"

"At least until we know what's going on."

Ruth fiercely gripped the canoe with both hands, her knuckles white. She spit out a stream of water. "*I* know what's going on. We . . . We're . . . We're being shot at."

"We're inside the city limits. It's illegal to shoot guns inside the city limits."

"What a consolation. Like a murderer would worry about breaking the law. I think I lost my sandals. I don't know. I can't feel my feet."

Helma kept the canoe between them and the rest of the lake. The shots seemed to have come from an area at the north end of the park. She slowly kicked backward, staying low, dragging the canoe—and Ruth—toward shore. Silence and peace settled over the lake again, an accusatory peace as if Helma certainly had imagined the shots.

"Thank God for this life vest," Ruth said.

"It might be more reasonable to thank me," Helma reminded her.

"I would if you hadn't been such a bully about it."

Helma touched bottom, her feet sliding on the slippery rocks beneath her. "Let's stay right here. You can put your feet down but don't stand up."

The rowboat in the center of the lake was advancing toward them, oars wide and splashing. On the dock, someone in orange waved, calling out in a voice like a bee's buzz. And in the distance Helma heard a siren.

"That can't be for us, can it?" Ruth asked. "Not so soon." Her lips were approaching the same shade of purple as her life vest.

At the distant boat ramp Helma spotted a familiarly shaped person jump from a dark car, leaving the driver's door open, and head hurriedly toward the path around the lake.

"This is one time when it pays to be under surveillance," Helma said, nodding toward the round figure bobbing their way.

"If I live, I might kiss him," Ruth said.

A police car shot into sight along the portion of road visible from the lake. Helma gratefully watched it approach, noting also the motorcycle that passed it, traveling at a high rate of speed in the opposite direction.

Detective Carter Houston reached them first, crashing through the alder trees and thimbleberry bushes that edged the shore, exhibiting admirable speed and disregard for his appearance.

"I didn't do it," Ruth said when she saw his red face.

He ignored her. Puffing, he hooked one suited arm around an angled tree trunk and leaned out over the water. Helma stared, certain that *was* a mixture of concern and relief crossing his face. "Were either of you hit? Are you all right?"

"I'm freezing and I lost my sandals," Ruth said. "*And*, I nearly drowned."

"Did you see who it was?" Helma asked him.

"I couldn't . . ." Carter Houston suddenly steadied

himself, as if he were mentally tidying up. He put on his bland face. "It'll be investigated, I assure you."

"Then will you stop talking and get me on dry land?" Ruth demanded.

Water fell away from Ruth in sheets as she climbed onto the bank and wrapped her arms around herself, her clothes clinging, her hair dripping. She was shaking uncontrollably.

"Miss Zukas?" the detective asked, holding out his hand.

"If you'll help me right my canoe, I'll paddle back to the dock."

"Don't be stupid, Helm," Ruth chattered at her. "It's not safe. What if he's still out there?"

"I'm certain the police have frightened him off," Helma said. "And it'll be easier to paddle my canoe back than to carry it."

"You just don't want to leave it in anybody else's hands," Ruth accused.

"No, I don't," Helma agreed.

"If you get pneumonia, it's your own fault."

Without hesitation, Detective Houston, in his shiny black shoes, stepped off the bank into ankle-deep water and helped her right her canoe and climb in, even giving it a push into the lake. "Stay close to the shore," he warned.

She nodded and paddled swiftly and competently beneath the overhanging tree branches, her motions warming her cold muscles, working up a light sweat that mingled with the drenching lake water by the time she beat Detective Houston and Ruth to the boat ramp and dock, where now two police cars waited.

Chief Wayne Gallant stood at the end of the dock, a blanket under his arm, watching her approach. "Nice canoe," he said, and hunkered down to reach for the bow deck, holding it close to the dock, at the same time touching a finger to the chipped gunwale.

"Thank you," Helma said. Her hair must be skintight

wet to her head. Not even a cap to protect her this time. "I believe we were shot at."

Helma got out and Chief Gallant wrapped the blanket around her shoulders, holding it there overlong while she clumsily tried to pull the edges together with her shaking hands. "That's what I understand. I'm relieved you're okay. Could you tell where the shots came from?"

"The north end of the park, I think. It was apparently a rifle, from that distance. Two shots. One skimmed a gunwale, but I didn't see anyone, or the glint of sunshine on metal." Waves of cold rose upward through her body, sinking beneath her flesh to her bones.

The chief nodded toward two policemen and they headed off toward the north. "As efficiently observant as usual, Helma."

"I try to be. Did the detective call you?"

"I was just heading to Seattle for a meeting." The chief studied the canoe, then swept his eyes around the lake.

Helma pulled the blanket tighter around herself and crouched, examining the gunwale. The bullet had chipped the outer rail, notching out a quarter-inch of wood. "This has to be repaired," she said aloud. "It's not a structural problem—yet, but it's unsight . . ."

"Why do you think someone would shoot at you?" the chief asked.

"It wasn't necessarily me. It may have been Ruth."

"And why do you suspect it was Ruth?"

"I didn't say I 'suspected' Ruth; I was only expressing there were two of us in the canoe. But you might learn more if you spoke to Ruth—and believed her."

"Have you been doing a little investigation on your own, Helma? Anything that might put you in danger that you should share with the police?"

"My 'investigation,' as you call it, is no secret from you, I'm sure. I wouldn't interfere with police procedure," Helma assured him, ignoring his expression. "This should remove Ruth from your list of suspects in the Joshman Lotz murder."

"Why? How is this incident connected to Lotz's murder?"

"Don't *you* believe it is? It's an extreme response to Ruth, who happened to see the murder victim and his brother quarreling immediately prior to his death. Her garage was burned. She's been threatened. And now this. To me, it's an indication that Ruth has information that could implicate someone else. You should be looking elsewhere for murder suspects."

Helma couldn't stop shivering. Chief Gallant offered her another blanket. She shook her head.

"Maybe it's someone on a rival Snow to Surf team jealous of that canoe."

"How did you know I was participating in the race?" Helma asked.

"Who's who on the Snow to Surf teams is a hot topic right now. The police department has a team, too."

A siren approached, and an ambulance entered the park, lights flashing.

"An ambulance?" Helma asked.

He looked at her with an expression held deep in his eyes, an expression Helma couldn't read. "I didn't know what we were dealing with. You might have been injured."

Ruth, dripping and shivering, accompanied by Detective Houston, whose shoes slogged and slurped with each step, appeared from the woodsy trail. Chief Gallant handed her a blanket and she huddled inside, miserably bedraggled. Detective Houston stood beside her, his mouth pursed, staring down at his ruined shoes.

🌿 chapter twelve 🌿

PADDLE TROUBLE

The police took Ruth home, but Helma insisted on driving her own car back to the Bayside Arms, shivering, the blanket still draping her shoulders and the heat and inside defoggers turned on full blast.

After showering and changing into dry clothes, she wasn't surprised to discover Walter David near the carports. He held his white Persian cat in his arms. "Let me put Moggy inside and I'll help you," he said.

She waited until they'd safely stored her canoe in the empty apartment before she asked, "Did you have a pleasant ride on your motorcycle this evening?"

Walter David turned too fast toward Helma. His eyes shifted above her head, Adam's apple visibly jumping. "Fine," he said. "It was fine."

"It's always a pleasant drive to Lake Pointer, I think. Although this evening wasn't as pleasant as other evenings."

Walter David fussed with the bow end of her canoe, lining it up with a carpet seam. He cleared his throat.

"Do you own a rifle?" Helma asked.

"It wasn't me!" Walter David shifted from foot to foot; his mouth spasmed.

"What wasn't you?" Helma asked pleasantly.

Walter David threw up his hands, a stressed man surrendering. "Okay. I went for a ride on my bike. Hearing you mention Lake Pointer reminded me of how long it had been since I'd been out there, so that's where I went."

"And?"

"I was at the park feeding the ducks . . ." Helma frowned and the manager amended, "Okay, I was *thinking* about feeding the ducks and I heard the gunshots and saw your canoe go over."

"But I saw you leave while we were still in the water."

He scuffed at a half-moon-shaped stain on the carpet. "A pickup pulled out of the end of the park like it was in a hurry, you know, spraying gravel and fishtailing. So I followed it. Tried to, anyway. The police cars got in the way and I lost it. Might have just been kids. I don't know."

"Can you describe the pickup?"

"Just a pickup. Full size."

"What color?"

"I don't know. I'm kinda color blind. A light tone."

"But you didn't see the driver?"

He shook his head. "Only the truck pulling out of the park."

"And you thought it drove away suspiciously fast, as if the driver wanted to get away from the area?"

"Maybe. You're making me feel like I'm in a courtroom, Helma." He laughed nervously. "Can I call my lawyer?"

"I apologize," Helma told him. "I always attempt to understand life's problems as clearly as possible."

"Yeah. I guess getting shot at is a problem. Who do you think it was? Somebody connected with the dead guy?"

"What makes you ask that?"

Walter David shrugged. "Your friend Ruth told me she was a suspect. Maybe somebody believes she did it and wants to get even with her."

"That's possible. Even people we consider most despicable have friends and champions," Helma pondered aloud, wondering if there might have been information gained from observing who attended Joshman Lotz's funeral, after all. "How long have you lived in Bellehaven?" she asked Walter David.

"My parents moved here when I was about three. From Iowa. I graduated from Bellehaven High. Even spent a year up at the college—I was all fired up to go into computers but the calculus requirement culled me out."

"Did you know Joshman Lotz, the man who was murdered?"

"No. But I remember when his daughter died."

"Catherine Lötz?" Helma asked in surprise. "How could you? You would have been a toddler."

Walter David hiked up his jeans and leaned against the wall between the living room and kitchen. "I was six. My mom had taken me to the park at Lake Wickersham. When a kid sees something like that, they never forget it."

"You saw her drown?"

Walter David shook his head. "Not the drowning itself. I didn't see her body when they brought it ashore either, but there was a lot of commotion. People running and crowding and pointing into the lake. Everything in a weird slow motion. And crying. The kids and the adults, too. My mother cried all the way home."

The were both silent, picturing the tragic scene unfolding on the pleasant beach.

"The paper said she swam out too far."

"My mother told my father, 'She just kept swimming.' "

Helma straightened and brushed her hands together as if they were dusty. "I appreciate your helping with my canoe, Walter. Good evening."

In her apartment, Helma scraped the golden skin and head of the last smoked chub into Boy Cat Zukas's dish, leaving the dish inside her apartment while she glanced through the *Bellehaven Daily News* on her balcony. Boy Cat Zukas crouched on the roof and glowered down at her, sniffing at the fishy odor emanating through her screen door.

There was no mention of the Joshman Lotz investigation in the paper, nothing more about the burning of Ruth's garage. On the bottom of the front page was a story about two people who'd dressed in skeleton costumes and set off stink bombs in the new mall, shouting that the mall was murdering downtown. "Shoppers applauded at first," the paper said, "thinking it was a promotional stunt for a new movie."

It was eight o'clock and still light. Long wisps of clouds high in the sky reflected pink undersides, violet tops, the water of the bay beneath them a soft silver. A low line of solid gray spread along the southwest horizon. Weather coming in. This would probably be the last colorful sunset for a few days.

A 'pale' pickup, Walter David had said. Light blue? Helma wondered just how extensively Chief Gallant had investigated Radio Kraft. Certainly the police had already interviewed him. It was Radio Kraft the police should have under surveillance.

Although Helma normally considered her options and any consequences at length before she took action, she also believed that when she was moved by a strong sense of righteousness or wonder, it was imperative to *act*. There was nothing impetuous about it; her unconsciousness was capable of compressed, comprehensive deliberation which if she were to do consciously would consist of days of thorough and careful consideration.

She appraised the now slate-colored clouds and fading sunset. It was dark enough that she could drive undetected to Sunspot Acres and just glance—take one quick peek—at Radio Kraft's pickup for any identifying oddities—such as a dented door or fuzzy dice—Walter David might recollect.

The hat Helma had worn to Lake Pointer was forever gone but on the top shelf of her closet she found another brimmed hat that tipped just so over her forehead, partially shading her face.

As she made a move to close and lock her balcony door, Boy Cat Zukas leapt from the roof to her balcony railing and issued two sharp and insistent meows.

Helma shoved the bowl of chub debris onto the balcony and locked the glass door before Boy Cat Zukas had crossed her balcony floor.

A single light hung tipsily from a pole in the rough parking lot of Sunspot Acres. The glow of lamps and flickering of televisions shone from a few of the apartment windows.

Helma pulled in, not too tentatively, not too purposefully, pretending she was coming home, that she lived in Sunspot Acres—a disturbing thought—but Helma had discovered long ago that people rarely noticed or censored what another person did with impunity. It was the cautious and uncertain who were caught, not those who acted as if they had the right and the privilege.

Believing so, she pulled into the space directly to the right of the pickup she remembered as Radio Kraft's. A heavily-built pale blue Ford. A web of cracks radiated from a round hole in the windshield on the passenger's side. Helma opened her door and stepped out, glancing casually into the truck bed. Whatever had been there was gone now. A coil of rope and a neatly folded blue tarp lay on the ridged metal floor. Nothing else. Despite the age of the truck it was very clean, even the hubcaps.

"What are you nosing around for?"

Helma spun around. Radio Kraft leaned against the rear fender of her Buick, a cigarette in his mouth, his long hair slicked back. In the weak light, he appeared larger than she remembered, his broken nose lumpily shadowed.

"I'm examining your truck to verify whether it's one I saw at Lake Pointer earlier this evening."

"And what if it is?"

"It would be a coincidental situation."

Radio Kraft took a long pull on his cigarette, his eyes narrowing. "I think you'd better get the hell out of here before I call the cops."

Helma leaned against the fender of Radio's pickup and crossed her arms in a more refined imitation of Radio Kraft.

"It wouldn't disappoint me if you did so. I might inform them of the person who witnessed a truck like this leaving Lake Pointer rather hurriedly after two shots were fired at my canoe."

"Listen, lady. What exactly is it you want? Why keep butting into my business?"

"My friend's suspected of murdering your brother."

"Then she oughta go to jail, shouldn't she? Maybe hang. They still do that here in Washington."

"I'm aware of that. You know she didn't do it."

"No I don't." He looked hard at Helma and she sensed him struggling to maintain control.

"I think you and your brother quarreled and you killed him yourself and now you're trying to blame the murder on an innocent woman."

Radio Kraft spit a bubbly wad on the ground a few inches from Helma's foot. She checked to be sure her shoes were clean but she didn't move.

"I spoke to Doctor Robertson, your other brother," Helma tried.

"Old Doc Footsie?" Kraft asked. "I'll bet he pretended he'd never heard of us, didn't he? Found under a cabbage leaf."

"Something like that," Helma said. "You didn't get along?"

Kraft snorted.

"What kind of father was Lotz?"

A different form of irritation passed over Radio's face. "Piss poor," he said so quickly Helma knew she'd caught Radio Kraft off guard and he'd answered without thinking.

"I know about his son he adopted out and his drowned daughter."

"Tough luck," Radio Kraft commented coolly.

"Wasn't it, though."

He threw his cigarette on the gravel and ground it

with his heel. "I want you out of here lady, just as fast as you can get your ass back in your car and if you know what's good for you, you'll quit snooping around."

"I'd like to warn you as well, or I assure you I'll do exactly as *I* said. And I *am* leaving, but not because you told me to. This conversation has obviously reached the limits of whatever heights it had been rising to and has now degraded into grunts and squeals."

Helma resolutely turned her back and got into her Buick without another glance at Radio Kraft, thinking once she felt his breath on the back of her neck and the mingling of his shadow with hers.

Every move she made was deliberate; pushing down her lock button before she fastened her seatbelt, stepping on the brake before she turned on the engine, looking behind her before she backed out. She drove away from Sunspot Acres as carefully and purposefully as she had driven there.

Helma set the box containing the red high-top sneakers on the counter in Shoes! Shoes! Shoes! The store was empty except for three teenage girls giggling over a display of spike-heeled sling-backs.

The bored girl at the cash register cracked her gum and asked, "Help you?"

"I'd like to exchange these shoes," Helma told her. She was thinking a pair of plain white deck shoes would be nice, the kind with leather laces and a good sole.

The girl lifted the lid and looked inside. "Got a receipt?"

"No, I don't. They were a gift."

"To *you*?" she asked, her eyes widening.

"Yes. Is that a problem?"

"No. But yeah, I can see why you'd want to exchange them."

"Why?" Helma asked.

The girl had the courtesy to blush. "I don't know. Not too many older people buy shoes like these."

Helma studied the red shoes. Ruth had said the high-top style was a sensible choice for canoeing. The salesgirl cracked her gum again and tapped her lacquered fingernails on the counter.

"You misunderstand me," Helma said coolly but politely. "It's the color of the shoes I wish to exchange, not the style."

"Helma," Ruth said, "there's this great party I have to attend tonight. You've *got* to come."

"You *have* to attend?"

"Uh-huh. It's the local art crowd. Some book people, too; right up your alley."

"I prefer to go to bed early tonight. Our team is practicing hand-offs tomorrow."

"What time?"

"Noon."

"Then it's no excuse. You can sleep in. But listen, if you'll come I promise we'll leave by eleven. It's a tame party, honest. No crazed gunmen or dead bodies or burning buildings. Even Detective Houston would have a good time. Boring. You'll love it. I need the publicity for my show."

"You've been receiving quite an amount of publicity lately."

"But this will be legit."

The party was in a converted church on the more bohemian edge of the "slope," closer to the college. Helma stood inside the old nave, orienting herself in the fusion of familiar and profane. The walls between the stained-glass windows were covered by murals of bright fanciful creatures and plants similar to the lurid covers of science fiction novels. The kitchen commanded the pulpit area and above her, the bedroom occupied the old choir loft. Kites hung from the high arched ceiling, swaying over the heads of the crowd like hovering birds of prey. Music issued from speakers somewhere above Helma, but mostly what she heard over the laughter and talk was a heartbeat of percussion.

"Isn't this great?" the towering purple Ruth asked

Helma, sweeping her arm around the pulsing interior.

Helma's dress didn't conform to that favored by the other attendees. She wore a beige skirt and pleated white blouse with a maroon vest Aunt Em had knit, and clip-on pearl earrings. In the swirling, colorful crowd of black and peacock hues and fist-size dangling earrings, Helma was an oasis of order and reason.

Ruth was soon surrounded by people she knew and Helma didn't, leaving Helma to make her arduous and circuitous way toward the food tables, catching snatches of unconnected conversation.

"I for one prefer her watercolors."

"No! *Who* gave him a grant?"

"Last I heard, he was mired down in big fluffy clouds. It's the Prozac, I tell you."

"I'd go for it if I could be sure of a tax write-off."

She poured herself a plastic cup of 7-Up and stood beneath a stained-glass window, surveying the chattering crowd. Helma didn't *dislike* parties; it was only that frequently in a crowd she was overcome by a kind of tunnel vision, unable to take in a roomful of people without becoming dizzily disoriented.

"Hey!" a male voice said close to Helma's ear. "It's one of the hotshots from the library. Canoe, right?"

Helma looked into the mildly glazed eyes of the man beside her. He held a plastic glass of beer pushed inside another empty glass. Blond, his body pulsing and bobbing to the music's beat. He looked familiar but then, because she served the public, many people did.

"I beg your pardon?"

"The barbecue in the park a couple weeks ago? Connie introduced us. I'm Al, canoeist supreme for the planning department. Good to see you." He thrust his free hand at Helma, shaking hers exuberantly.

"Helma Zukas," she said.

"Connie said you're going solo."

"Yes, I am."

"Anybody tell you the canoe leg's eighteen miles long? You'll be lucky if you make eight by yourself."

"I'm training."

Al the canoeist supreme snorted. "That's rich. Too bad you're not our only competition: we could tie our paddles behind our backs and still win." He took two swallows of beer and looked over Helma's head. "Great party, huh? I don't often come to this kind of gig."

"I believe you. Will you excuse me?"

"You bet. See you at the race. Don't bother to train on our account!"

Protecting her 7-Up, Helma moved a few feet closer to the table, enough to separate herself irrevocably from Al.

"You're from the library, aren't you?"

Helma turned in dread but this time she recognized the flamboyant woman in front of her, Rebecca Fredericks Shaw, a Bellehaven mystery author. The library owned all her books although Helma hadn't read them.

"Hello," Helma said. "We just purchased your new book a few weeks ago."

Too late, she wished she'd said something else, knowing what Rebecca Fredericks Shaw would ask next—if she'd read her latest offering. Helma furiously searched for a way to deflect the question. At that moment, she spotted Howard Manly, another Bellehaven writer and a frequent patron of the library. She smiled and eagerly beckoned him to join them.

"Miss Zukas," Howard Manly said, smiling.

"You know Howard Manly, of course," she said to Rebecca Fredericks Shaw. "I'm sure you two," Helma said, gesturing between the two authors, "must have a lot in common, with both of you publishing new books this year."

Howard Manly and Rebecca Fredericks Shaw smiled distantly and uneasily at one another, simultaneously sipping at their drinks. Helma was puzzled until it suddenly dawned on her that neither had read the other's work and she herself hadn't read either one of them.

"What do you think of the rumor that a new chain bookstore is moving to Bellehaven?" she hastily asked.

With relief and eagerness the three launched into an animated conversation on the evil ways of conglomerates.

In a book titled *Uncomfortable Situations*, Helma had read that while attending a party, if an uncomfortable person were to find a place to sit, hold a glass of liquid and look approachable, people—many of them not comfortable at parties either—would naturally gravitate toward him or her.

So that's exactly what she did and that's exactly what happened and she was surprised to glance at her watch, wondering if it was eleven o'clock yet, to discover it was twenty minutes to midnight.

"I believe it would be more efficient if I began running as you approached the hand-off line rather than wait for you to cross it," Helma told Jeffrey, the bicyclist/circulation page after their first fumbled attempt. "The instant our speeds match, pass the wristband to me."

"I'll be going pretty fast," Jeffrey said.

"So will I," Helma assured him.

They stood in the drizzly afternoon on a low-maintenance paved road a hundred yards from the bank of the Nitcum River. Even in the drizzle and gray light, all the rich spring growth tinged the air green. The river curving past reflected emerald and amber.

When Jeffrey cycled to the hand-off line, completing his leg of the race, Helma would snatch the wristband and race across a grassy field onto a rocky spit where her canoe would be waiting in an advantageous location. The only difficulty Helma anticipated was launching her canoe from the rocky shore.

She peered at the cottonwood trees and willow bushes that lined the banks of the Nitcum River, imagining someone hiding there, watching, intending harm.

"Ready to try again?" Jeffrey asked, turning the wheel of his bicycle.

Helma shuddered and put guns and murder and Radio Kraft out of her mind.

"Ready," she told Jeffrey, bouncing a little on the soles of her new pale blue high-top sneakers.

"Miss Zukas, Ruth Winthrop is asking if you'll come down to the police station."

"Is she under arrest?" Helma asked, turning off the stove burners under the dinner she was preparing from *Diet for Competitors*.

"Not at this time," came the detective's rather smug answer.

"Then why are you holding her?"

Detective Carter Houston sighed. "We're not holding Miss Winthrop; we asked to speak to her and she chose to come here."

"Regarding what matter?"

"Miss Zukas, shall I tell Ruth Winthrop you're unable to come to the station?"

"I'll be there in eight minutes."

Ruth sat in a small sparse room, occupying two chairs: one for herself and one for her feet. She jumped up when Detective Houston ushered Helma in.

"Where the hell have you been?" Ruth demanded.

"Practicing hand-offs. What's going on here?"

Ruth dropped back into her chair and shoved the other chair toward Helma with her foot. "They found the damnedest thing: a canoe paddle *buried* where I meant to put in snapdragons—or lavender—I forget. But *buried*. I thought it was pretty crazy but seeing as you're the canoe expert . . ."

"I buried it," Helma said, ignoring the chair. "I meant to tell you."

Detective Houston held up his hand, stopping Helma. "Wait a minute. I'll get the chief."

"Why?" Ruth challenged. "Won't he believe you or does he have to hear it straight from Helma's lips?"

When the detective left the room, Ruth said, "Joshman Lotz was probably whacked with that paddle."

"It's *mine*, I said," Helma reminded her. "That paddle

didn't touch Lotz. I *did* bury it. For a very good reason . . . "

"Save it until the Gestapo gets here."

"Detective Houston said *you* insisted on coming to the station, Ruth. Why?"

Ruth rocked in her chair. "I don't know. More appropriate atmosphere?"

"Or a chance for more publicity?"

"Helma Zukas! That's unfair. That paddle isn't all. Remember the gas can I kept in the trunk of my Saab 'cause the gas gauge was broken? It was found in the morning glory down the alley—empty of course. No one's fingerprints on it but yours truly."

That's not surprising," Helma told Ruth. "An arsonist would be more cunning than to leave fingerprints on the means of incineration. The police know that. What about Radio Kraft? Have you seen him?"

"Not in the flesh. I heard he took my name in vain down at Joker's. I don't *see* him but I get the feeling he's not too far away."

"Miss Zukas," Chief Gallant said, entering the room ahead of Detective Houston. "The detective here tells me you claim to be connected to the canoe paddle?"

"Yes. It's my bow paddle. It was warped."

Ruth, Chief Gallant, and Detective Houston looked at Helma expectantly.

"And?" the chief prompted.

"I buried it at Ruth's because the earth around my building is too rocky. Burying a hardwood paddle for a few days straightens the warp."

Detective Houston harrumphed, one side of his mouth drawn into a sneer.

"If you doubt my word, call my brother Bruce in Michigan who recently shipped my canoe and paddles to me. He can describe them, as well as explain traditional care of hardwood paddles."

"I don't find it necessary to phone your brother," Chief Gallant said. "But you can if you want, detective."

"I will," the detective said, folding his hands together on the table over his notebook.

"I don't suppose you have a story to explain away the gas can?" Ruth asked Helma.

"I'm afraid not. I believe you don't have much reason to keep Ruth any longer?" she asked Chief Gallant.

"She's been free to leave ever since she arrived," the chief said.

"I can give you a ride," Helma offered as she secured the strap of her purse over her shoulder.

Ruth shook her head. "These guys can see that I safely reach my little home. They wanted to talk to me; I'm their responsibility."

"Are you sure you know where to pick me up?" Helma asked Ruth.

"You've only told me four times and drawn a map besides. And if I *do* get lost I'm sure our personal detective or one of his minions will be somewhere nearby to rescue me."

The Nitcum River, deep brown and green, awaited Helma's trial run, whispering past with secret bubbles and splashes, faster than it appeared at first glance, assuredly faster and wider than Scoop River.

The Nitcum, after leaving the mountains, was rated Class I, a "teddy bear" of a river, her brother Bruce would have called it. Wide, with gentle curves and few rapids, rolling sedately through trees and farmland. But Helma had witnessed the Nitcum in flood, when an unexpected January thaw burst it over its banks, when it ferociously tore out trees and buildings and scoured the soil off the farmlands, racing wildly past, dragging debris and taking lives.

Helma's canoe was poised at the edge of the bank. Lying on its floor was a new waterproof stuff sack holding necessities, including a second hat, a first-aid kit, and duct tape. Her bailer and rope bag were looped over the stern seat.

Ruth bent down and pulled a rock out of the mud near

Helma's canoe. "Did you get this thing bullet-proofed when you had the gunwale fixed?"

"Your humor's in poor taste, Ruth."

"So sorry."

Helma's training had progressed beyond the limits of Lake Pointer. She was fast; her strokes were strong and natural, her stamina superior. Every night she concentrated on exercises to increase the strength of her torso and arms: twisting and lifting, stretches and pulls. She was ready for the river.

"Don't forget, my car likes a little extra gas when you come out of a turn," Helma told Ruth. "It stalls sometimes."

"Got it, Helma."

"And don't park in the mud by the bridge."

"Okay."

"Watch the temperature gauge. It's never overheated but sometimes the needle advances. I stop and let the engine cool off, then."

"Am I the first stranger to drive your car?" Ruth asked, jangling Helma's car keys.

"In a long time."

"Well, I'm honored." She pointed to Helma's high-tops. "You might have been right. Those baby blues look better on you than the red. Here comes some sun. Sure you don't want my sunglasses?"

"No thanks." Helma didn't like the way sunglass lenses altered the colors of the world, preferring instead to turn her head from the sun's direct glare, or during Bellehaven's few sunny days, to wear an adequately brimmed hat. Today, besides her brimmed hat, she wore long cotton sleeves and PF-15 sunscreen.

"Okay then," Ruth said, adjusting her sunglasses. "Avast ye. Watch out for white whales and albatrosses. I'll see you at Frango Bridge in a couple of hours."

Helma waved and with one foot in the center of her canoe, pushed off into the little eddy beside the bank, launching slightly upstream. She'd bought a sleeping bag pad and cut out a rectangle to fit in the bottom of her canoe to protect her knees. She'd briefly considered glueing it in for stability, but she couldn't face slathering glue onto the glowing wood.

She settled in awkwardly, the canoe rocking and wallowing, feeling trembly, sensing beneath her and through her paddle as her canoe swung out into the river and was carried downstream, the force and speed and power of the water nothing like Lake Pointer. She, Helma Zukas, was suddenly very small, the cedar hull of her canoe unbearably thin.

She concentrated, pulling with the river on each stroke, not fighting it, carried along, matching her pitiful sliver of power to the Nitcum's majestic, relentless movement. She rode the river, steadily guiding her canoe into the center of the main current, speed increasing so effortlessly and . . . helplessly.

Gradually, Helma's taut muscles began to relax and she felt once again that curious connection between body and river, an *extension* of herself as if its heart and hers drew together to beat in deep concurrence.

She took her eyes from the silky center of the main current and took in the banks where logjams lurked and branches overhung, daring to trap unwary canoeists or kayakers. She slipped into a cool bar of shade as she paddled beneath a steel bridge, cars rumbling above her.

The Nitcum turned away from the road and now the only sounds were the currents and ripples and the movement of her paddle. Ahead of her, she spotted a lone kayaker rounding a curve, double paddle turning.

A deer raised its head and its eyes met Helma's. They watched each other so long her canoe began to slip broadside. She straightened herself and continued on.

The current V'd slightly and beyond its point, a long babble of gentle rapids ridged into wider water and then flattened serenely again. She slowed until the kayaker had gone through and out of sight, then Helma moved closer to the midline of her canoe and nimbly passed through the rapids, keeping her bow straight, careful not to bump her paddle against the rocks. She smiled.

The river flowed past a pasture of Holstein cows that took no notice of Helma, even when she sounded a low "moo" at them.

A mile farther and she began tentatively to sing, "Row, row, row your boat." Long ago, in St. Alphonse, Sister Mary Martin had pointed her clicker at Helma during practice for the Christmas pageant and said, "Wilhelmina, move your lips but make no sound." Now, after the fourth round of "Row, row, row your boat," Helma took a deep breath and burst loudly into a rendition of that long-ago aborted "O, Come All Ye Faithful."

She paddled rhythmically, using her body and relaxing between each pull as Uncle Tony had taught her, knowing she'd have far better success in the upcoming race if she maintained a steady pace than if she attempted bursts of speed that would surely burn her out too fast.

A crow cawed, then another, landing on the black bank ahead of her and tearing at a dead fish. Behind them, pink wild roses bloomed among the brambles.

She couldn't say when it began but the current had carried her into a narrower, deeper, quieter stretch of water when she grew aware of a gnawing unease invading her pleasure. It wasn't concern for her canoe; the wooden craft was completely dry and moving with its usual graceful ease. She squinted downstream. The kayaker who'd been ahead of her earlier wasn't in sight. Behind her, upstream, the river was empty. Light from the intermittent sun lit the water, concealing its color.

She studied the dense growth on either side of the river, deep green leaves swaying in the rising and falling breeze, the verdant gloom behind the trees, the muddy banks. No sounds, no unusual movements. But still, she was uncomfortable, and more than uncomfortable, groundlessly fearful.

Ahead, a stand of willow grew close to the river, hanging graceful branches over deep water. Helma cut out of the main current and paddled into the willow, avoiding a log and peering into the slower water for branches just beneath the surface.

Inside the yellow-green cascade of willow surrounding her like a waterfall, she clung close to the sandy bank, reaching for a solid, knobby limb that had grown out parallel to the river, wrapping her arm around it and steadying herself while she stilled her heart, listening. Water fingering through the branches, a tentative bird call, an airplane droning in the distance. An iridescent dragonfly darted past. She turned her head, upstream, downstream, careful not to move her canoe.

There was nothing there. Nothing. But Helma sensed another presence, not benign. "James Dickey, where are you when you're needed?" she whispered.

After several minutes of silent watching and waiting, Helma chided herself, doubting her usually dependable senses. The willow branches undulated gracefully around her in a pale curtain. She couldn't sit there all day.

Using the branches, she moved to the outer edge of the willow, bow pointing downstream. She took a deep breath and angled out toward the Nitcum's main current, paddling the silent Indian stroke with all her strength.

She didn't drift or pause or study the riverbanks again. Kneeling in the bottom of her canoe, her knees wide and braced against the sides, she paddled in long graceful strokes that fairly skimmed her canoe down the river.

Perspiration slid down her back and between her breasts. Her shoulders ached and her thighs cramped. But even after the feeling of danger left her, she continued the grueling pace until Frango Bridge appeared before her like Oz and she gratefully pulled into the shallows beside the bridge where Ruth sat in the sand, holding a pen and a magazine folded backward.

The bow nudged the sand and Helma raised her paddle, exhausted and sick to her stomach.

Ruth grabbed the canoe. "Wow. Great time, Helm. You look beat. Better save it for the race."

Helma slowly and painfully unfolded herself, rubbing her calves and thighs. "Did you see a kayak go past a few minutes ahead of me?"

"Last I saw were three college kids whooping it up in a rubber raft about twenty minutes ago."

"No, this was a single person."

"Who was it?"

"I don't know," Helma told her. "He must have pulled out farther back."

"Nothing unusual about that, is there?" Ruth asked.

"No."

Ruth looked both ways on the river, frowning. "Did you run into trouble, Helm?" she asked, her face calmly serious.

"No. Nothing happened. It was a feeling I had. Maybe I'm just easily spooked these days."

"Understandable. Sit down and have a drink of water."

They sat on Ruth's blanket while Helma drank half a bottle of water and rubbed her aching muscles, still checking upstream. She glanced at Ruth's magazine. With a ballpoint pen, Ruth was following a complicated maze.

"Ruth," Helma said. "You've started this maze at the finish instead of the beginning."

"It's too hard the other way."

A double kayak passed, then an aluminum boat. But no single kayaker.

chapter thirteen

WORDS ON WATER

"**A**nd then when I corralled those two in the kiddie reference area, it dawned on the other one he'd eaten too many cookies and needed to upchuck," Roberta said as she poured coffee into her insulated mug. She set down the pot and made sweeping outward motions from her open mouth. "While I was mopping *that* up, off he went to find a can of root beer."

"The remarkable recuperative abilities of youth," George Melville commented.

"Just wait until it's your turn to chaperone Camp-out in a Book," Roberta said, pointing her mug at him. "It's a good thing the next day is Sunday because you *need* a day off. I swear ten-year-olds don't sleep."

"At least they haven't progressed to other, more interesting activities available when they can't sleep."

"Hah!" Roberta answered. "I had my doubts about a couple of the girls. Very eager to share their misinformation."

"It's preposterous," Patrice said as she poured cream from her own private container into her coffee. "I refuse to have any part of it." She sniffed. "Children sleeping in the library. We'll be taking in the homeless next."

George Melville put his finger to his lips. "Don't give the Moonbeam any ideas."

150

"That is a disrespectful nickname, no matter your opinion of our director," Patrice said.

"You'd take part, if like the rest of us, you still had to worry about your job," Roberta said.

Patrice's eyes flashed with a glimmer of naughtiness. "At this stage, in the final weeks of my career, I suppose I could get away with whatever I wanted."

"Anarchy could reign, Patrice," George Melville agreed eagerly. "You could even bring in Bink . . ." He winced. "Sorry, I forgot."

Patrice lowered her head and turned without a word, carrying her cup to her cubicle, back straight, walking in overly tight steps.

"That woman's become a rebel since she decided to quit. If she keeps it up I might start to like her," George said.

"Go apologize," Roberta urged George, nudging him with her elbow.

"I did. Do you want me to grovel?"

"That would be novel."

Helma left the lounge with her tea and entered her own cubicle, discreetly leaving Patrice to her privacy but noting from the corner of her eye how Patrice sat slumped at her desk, her hands folded on her blotter, the photos of Binky arranged before her.

"Grief is also an opportunity," Patrice said aloud from her side of the bookshelves.

Helma didn't answer, suspecting Patrice was talking to herself and choosing not to embarrass the woman in her momentary lapse. Helma noiselessly set her tea on the cork pad that protected her desktop and opened a new book catalog titled *Wars of the World*.

"Endings become new beginnings. We change our old ways whether we intend to or not. It's a little like the Moonbeam's idea of reincarnation, isn't it? Only it's the living who reincarnate, not the dead."

When Helma heard Patrice say "Moonbeam," she *did* stand and peered over the shelves at Patrice, who now leaned back in her chair, smiling vaguely, twisting her glasses on their gold chain.

"Are you all right, Patrice?" Helma asked.

Patrice looked up at Helma. "Just thinking aloud. Life is curious, isn't it?"

"I've heard that."

"Here I go, leaving my lifelong home for Arizona and here you are, Helma Zukas, frolicking with a lot of teenagers to participate in a *race*."

"I don't believe there are any teenagers on the Snow to Surf team."

"Not in years, anyway. I used to canoe. Back in Camp Miklatooka in the San Juan Islands. My parents sent me there three glorious summers in a row. A lake camp on an island surrounded by the ocean. Oh, it was lovely, paddling along the lake shore by moonlight, the music of the hoot owl and bullfrog, the lapping water and misty shores."

Helma sniffed the air between their cubicles, wondering if somehow Patrice had slipped alcohol into her coffee.

"How I'd love to canoe again," Patrice said wistfully.

Afterward, Helma would puzzle over what possessed her but at that moment she was moved by this softer, sadder side of Patrice. "I'd be happy to take you out on Lake Pointer in my canoe," she told Patrice. "What about Thursday night?"

Patrice straightened herself in her chair. "That's my lapidary club night. Tomorrow evening would be preferable. I'll meet you at Lake Pointer, at the boat ramp, say seven o'clock-ish?"

"Unless it rains," Helma said, grasping for an excuse, experiencing the sinking regret of people who speak too hastily.

"It won't," Patrice told her assuredly.

As Helma walked through the public service area of the library on the way to the reference desk, Jeffrey, the Snow to Surf bicyclist/circulation page, passed. He suddenly whipped an overdue notice from the stack he was carrying and thrust it toward Helma the instant they passed each other. Helma deftly snatched it with her free hand.

Jeffrey stopped and beamed at Helma. "Just testing your reflexes," he said in a voice that brought curious stares from patrons standing at the computer catalogs. "Good recovery!"

Helma hadn't considered they might practice for the Snow to Surf Race within the library building itself.

"I've got something to show you," Ruth said. "Pick me up in case my house is bugged."

Helma hung up the phone and finished closing the foil packet of Kitty Treatums. Normally, she wouldn't have bought such frivolous food but they were a close-out special in the grocery store. Boy Cat Zukas *hadn't* left any small dead animals on her balcony in two weeks. On the other side of her sliding glass door, Boy Cat Zukas sat beneath the balcony light washing his paws, having gulped the treats as if they might escape.

"Where did you get these?" Helma asked Ruth, looking at the criminal records of Joshman Lotz and Carl "Radio" Kraft by the glow of her car's dome light.

"They're 'rap sheets.' "

"*You* went to the police station and requested them?"

Ruth shook her head. "I have friends within the inner circle."

"Who?"

"Remember Sidney Lehman, the boy in blue who found me so charming a few years ago?"

"I recall the first clause but not the second."

"Then you weren't paying attention. Anyway, he was only fulfilling a citizen's request. He even added a few details for us. Now the question is, which of these two brothers is the bigger slime ball?"

Helma skimmed the "rap sheets," as Ruth called them. Joshman Lotz had been five years older than his brother Carl "Radio" Kraft. Same mother, different fathers. Most of the crimes were petty but numerous, and by their corresponding dates, had obviously been committed at about the same time or in the company of one another. Assault, driving while intoxicated, breaking and entering, resisting arrest, disorderly conduct.

Joshman Lotz had gone to prison when he was caught inside a home by the returning owner, who'd nearly died in the ensuing fight.

"Look at this assault and disturbing the peace eighteen years ago," Ruth instructed. "Same dates. I bet they were fighting brother against brother. Banging each other around is *not* a new development."

"Here's one of Joshman Lotz's that's not so petty," Helma said. "Back in the sixties: indecencies with a minor runaway."

"Bad old sixties," Ruth commented.

"That doesn't excuse him."

"I wasn't implying it did."

"All of this only confirms what we already knew."

"I think," Ruth said, refolding the sheets, "that Joshman got sent up for the brothers' mutual crimes and that's what they were quarreling about when I walked into Joker's. Old Joshman was feeling a little cranky and took it out on me."

"And you were noticeable enough in your responses that you became the perfect suspect."

"Right."

"If Radio Kraft killed his brother, why would he tell people he wanted revenge on *you*? That only calls more attention to himself."

"Especially if I ended up dead. No, it's an act to throw off the cops. We're not exactly dealing with geniuses here."

"It's more likely you heard one of the brothers say something incriminating. And now Radio Kraft is trying to stop you from passing it on."

"I told you before. I don't have a clue what they were saying. I was totally not paying attention. Let's go turn him in."

Helma shook her head. "At this point I think the police doubt what either one of us say."

"Yeah. Your warped paddle story was pretty far out."

"It wasn't a story, Ruth. It's true. What do you intend to do with these criminal records?"

"Nothing. Just a little grease for the mill."

"You mean 'grist.' Mills grind grist. It's a word for grain."

Ruth thought a moment. "I like 'grease' better. It's less complicated."

"You could say 'grease the wheels,' but it's 'grist for the mill.' "

"Is it a law?"

"No, but if you consult a dictionary of cliches and idioms, you'll find 'grist for the mill' listed as a centuries-old idiom, meaning that there may be some useful information to be gleaned from a larger amount, like wheat separated from chaff."

Ruth, who rarely surrendered to proof she disagreed with, raised her chin and said, "I consider English a living language, and if I want to say 'grease for the mill,' I suppose I can."

"Don't expect to be understood, then."

"Well, *you* knew what I was talking about."

To Helma's left, as she exited Ruth's alley, a dark car was parked at the curb, the driver's outline visible in the gloomy shine from the streetlight.

Helma turned off her motor and set her brake. Then she removed her keys and stepped out into the dewy night air. Gravel crunched beneath her feet. The dog behind the fence of the Victorian house whined softly, then was silent, its nose pressed between the slats.

She didn't hesitate; her steps were resolute and even. She rounded the hood of the dark car and tapped on the driver's window.

The window was rolled down. At first Helma didn't recognize him with his dark glasses and the sandwich to his mouth.

"You saw me, huh?" he asked as he chewed. "The dark glasses didn't throw you off?"

It was Rock, the library patron and new security guard for "Security for You."

"Actually, dark glasses at night are an attention getter, not a disguise," Helma said. "What are you doing here?"

He glanced suspiciously up and down the dark street before answering. "On a job. Security for people on vacation. Stopped for a bite."

"You're checking houses in this neighborhood?"

"You got it. Make sure nobody's been messing around. People depend on me to keep their houses secure. Security: secure. Get it?"

Helma glanced around the car's interior, noting the radio and the box of Little Debbie strawberry cake rolls, wishing it were just a little lighter so she could see what was written on the clipboard lying on the passenger seat.

"Do you still live at Sunspot Acres?" Helma asked.

"I'm moving next week to Orca Ridge. They've got a pool."

Rock glanced at his watch and gave Helma a smart salute. "Better go now. I've got a job to do."

And he turned the ignition and slowly pulled away from the curb, his window still down, on to his next appointed round.

Helma already had her canoe in the water when Patrice arrived at precisely seven o'clock. As Patrice had promised, it unfortunately wasn't raining but it was cloudy. Helma had first driven through the park at Lake Pointer, checking for blue pickups, seeing none and hoping she and Radio Kraft had clearly understood one another. She'd also kept an eye on her rearview mirror for the presence of a plain dark blue car. But obviously Helma was of less interest to the police than Ruth.

"What a pretty little canoe," Patrice said, approaching the dock in navy polyester pants and a nautical-style shirt, her patent leather purse over her shoulder. "It looks homemade."

"It was made by an uncle who was a craftsman," Helma said, bristling at the way Patrice rolled the word "homemade."

"A Lithuanian craftsman?" Patrice asked with unnecessary emphasis.

"From Michigan."

"Hmm. Homemade paddles, too?"

"Only one. The other's a temporary I rented today, but you don't need to paddle."

"Oh no. I want to."

"You could lock your purse in my car," Helma suggested.

"No thank you. Thieves can rifle a car in seconds."

Patrice climbed into the bow end of the canoe with surprising agility. She tucked her purse beneath her seat and held the canoe steady to the dock while Helma got in.

They launched into the blue water and after a grim false start, coordinated their paddling with admirable efficiency, and Helma's canoe glided through the water.

"Ah, lovely, lovely," Patrice said after a few minutes, sounding so genuinely delighted, Helma wished she could see Patrice's face. The evening was calm; a slight breeze ruffled the treetops.

"Are you tired?" Helma asked. "Would you like to rest?"

"Not yet. Let's round the lake once and then drift a while."

They did just that. Helma occasionally scanned the shore for a blue pickup but sensed this evening was safe. Patrice's strokes were even and smooth, with just the right amount of depth and draw. Despite her apprehension Helma found she was enjoying herself, amazed that she and Patrice could be so well synchronized.

When they drifted to a stop in the center of Lake Pointer, Patrice turned sideways on the seat, smiling, not even visibly perspiring.

"You're a very good paddler," Helma complimented her.

"I was afraid I'd forgotten how. It must be like they say about bicycling. This really is a lovely canoe, Helma. Very sleek. What's this little door?" Patrice opened the small enclosed space beneath the heart-shaped bow deck.

"Uncle Tony added those to the girls' canoes. He said they were for our lipstick."

"A nice homey touch. You canoed often as a girl?" Patrice asked.

Helma nodded.

The bald eagle, one of a line that had been a presence for so many years, sat on its snag. Was it scrutinizing them, or did it disdainfully consider people of no interest, inedible and insignificant, no more than a lump in the scenery?

"I wonder if I'll miss this greenery, all this water," Patrice mused. "I've never lived where it's dry."

"Have you had any buyers interested in your house?" Helma asked her.

"A few. There's a couple from Spokane and a family from Seattle who both seem serious," Patrice said. "I'm personally leaning toward the family. They have a daughter who loves dogs."

"That would be a change for your house," Helma said. Patrice had shown very little tolerance for children over the years.

"I was the last child raised in it. It's about time for another one. Houses tend to get stuffy if they sit too long between children."

Being on open water did something to people, like late-night plane trips or riding the ferry. Artificial boundaries melted under the spell of the shared journey. Intimacy without commitment, with an enforced conclusion. It was easier to talk, to divulge. On land, Helma never would have asked what she did next.

"Had you wanted children?"

Patrice had been married once as a young woman,

everyone in the library knew that. Helma had tried, but failed to envision the man who'd shared a brief life with Patrice.

Instead of growing huffy, as Helma expected, Patrice sighed and trailed her fingers in the water. "No. Well, once, briefly. It was just as well, I suppose, seeing that my marriage didn't last. There are already too many children from broken homes."

"I see many single mothers who do admirable jobs raising their children alone."

"I don't believe I would have been one of them. And you, Miss Zukas," Patrice asked, stressing the "Miss," "did you want children?"

"I never considered it. A husband seemed a prerequisite to me."

"A husband's no guarantee—not of children nor of happiness."

Helma waited, not expecting gossip, rather hoping Patrice would divulge more, but instead Patrice began discussing the advantages of Tucson's dry climate over Bellehaven's. "I may even take up golf," Patrice said. "I've heard it's good insurance against arthritic shoulders."

Helma's Aunt Em had claimed that milking cows was good for her arthritic hands, keeping a cow for just that reason long after she and Uncle Mark had quit farming.

They drifted, watching ripples rise on the water, lulled by the relative silence. Dozy birds twittered in the trees, voices called as picnickers packed up. Helma held her paddle lazily across her knees and watched the lights along the park's drive blink on.

"It's getting dark," Helma finally said. "We'd better go in."

"I suppose we should. Incidentally, I've heard the rumors about your friend being under suspicion for Joshman Lotz's murder."

"It's only temporary."

"The police will find the real criminal soon, I'm sure."

She paused and Helma leaned forward, hearing the hesitation in Patrice's voice, waiting.

"The boy, the Lotz baby?" Patrice said. "I know who adopted him. The adoption *was* closed, but secrets get out."

Still Helma waited, her breath held.

"I don't suppose it's of any significance to the case, but my mother told me he went to a family in Dallas. I remember their name because it was so apropos for that time: McCarthy."

"Do you know where he is now?"

Patrice shook her head. "Nothing except the name of the people who adopted him."

They paddled silently back to the dock, as swiftly and fluently as they'd paddled around the lake. Helma pondered the relevance of the adopted baby, considering what to do with the information besides add it to the growing evidence in her spiral notebook. McCarthy. She felt a chill of discomfort, remembering her U.S. history of the 1950s.

As she reached for the dock cleat, Helma kicked Patrice's purse, spilling the contents on the floor of her canoe. The little craft rocked and tilted as they both scrambled for coins, tissues, and wallet in the gloom.

"I'm sorry," Helma said.

"You were right. I should have left it in the car." She laughed briefly. "A patent leather purse *is* incongruous in a canoe, isn't it?" Patrice paused before getting out of the canoe, holding up a round object. "I'd like to give this to you, Helma."

"What is it?"

"It's a good luck coin."

Patrice placed the cool object in Helma's hand and Helma sensed this was an unplanned moment, that Patrice was uncomfortable, maybe even regretful of what she was doing.

"My uncle gave this to me when I was a girl," Patrice said. "It's from the 1933 Century of Progress Exposition in Chicago. One of those silly things you begin to carry for no reason and after a while you feel responsible for. Maybe it'll help on the race." She laughed shortly. "You'll *need* luck."

"Thank you, Patrice. That's very kind of you."

"Actually, it's a relief to be rid of it."

Patrice tried to help Helma replace the canoe on the Buick's rack. Their coordination was gone. They bumped into each other and dangerously tipped the canoe toward the graveled ramp approach and then the Buick's windshield and got in one another's way.

"I think I've got it," Helma said. "Go ahead and step back."

"We do seem to be muddling it up, don't we?" Patrice said, obliging.

Leaving the canoe and Lake Pointer put both Helma and Patrice squarely back on land again. Their brief personal exchange in the middle of Lake Pointer might never have taken place.

"It was kind of you to take me for a ride in your little boat," Patrice said formally, holding her purse like the Queen of England as Helma tied the last half hitch.

"You're welcome," Helma said.

They each climbed into their respective cars, fastened their seatbelts, and drove home.

❧ chapter fourteen ❧

SHADOWS

Helma first snipped out the president's head from the cover of *Time* magazine, followed by a less flattering inset of the First Lady. She admired the two busts lying on her coffee table in scalpeled perfection, then, not having an interest in beginning a file folder for political personalities, she crumpled the smiling faces and threw them in the trash along with the ruined cover and scraps of shiny paper.

That done, she phoned Police Chief Wayne Gallant. "I recently learned information that could be significant to the Lotz investigation," Helma told him.

"Can you tell me now or would you feel more comfortable coming into the office?" the chief asked.

"Now is fine. I discovered that Joshman Lotz's infant son was adopted by a family in Dallas, Texas, named McCarthy."

The chief was silent.

"I know that's not very specific to go on, but with computers and modern techniques . . ."

When the chief remained silent, Helma asked, "You already know this, don't you?"

"Normally," Chief Gallant said deliberately, "I wouldn't confirm or deny, but considering your tendency to launch inquiries of your own and wanting to save you the expense of long distance calls or hours of frustration, I'll tell you we located the son. We know where he was the night Lotz died."

"He gave you an alibi?" Helma asked, loath to abandon her theory so soon.

"No. It wasn't necessary. But Helma, he's leading a happy and responsible life. He knows nothing of his background except that he was adopted and has no interest in pursuing his biological parents. This is one time I prefer to let the facts remain secret."

"Oh."

"Don't you agree?"

"You're sure about his alibi?"

"Completely."

"All right." As she spoke, Helma took a pencil from the holder beside the phone and reluctantly crossed out two lines in her notebook.

"How are your preparations for the Snow to Surf Race going?" Wayne Gallant asked.

"Very well." Helma had a sudden thought. "You're not on the police department's team, are you?"

"Not this year. But I heard we've got a pretty good team."

"That's exactly what I've heard said about the library's team," Helma replied.

"What kind of security is that?" George Melville asked as he scrutinized the plate of shrimp puffs and chose the largest one. "A twenty-four-hour guard, my own lock on the door, climate controlled, well-lit, and the damn place gets broken into anyway."

"What did they take?" Helma asked. She herself took a spinach and feta cheese delicacy created by Roberta. It was Eve's birthday and like other staff events and holidays, the table in the lounge was laden with food. "Nobody can beat librarians for food parties," Ruth had commented once on hearing of another celebration in the library. "You guys must *read* those cookbooks."

"Only the most valuable pieces, naturally. My grandfather's grandmother clock. A bentwood rocker, a marble-topped chest. Pieces too big for my apartment so I decided to store them somewhere safe. Hah!"

"Don't you mean your grandmother's grandfather clock?" Eve asked. Her pink paper crown was in danger of slipping from her head into the bowl of lavender/lemonade punch. "Or maybe your grandfather's grandmother's clock?"

"No, my dear, I mean my grandfather's grandmother clock. It's like a grandfather clock, you know, only smaller, daintier."

"That's kinda sexist."

"They didn't know that back then."

Roger and Ms. Moon entered the lounge and began filling paper plates. Helma had brought raw vegetables and an onion dip from the deli.

"When was the last time you checked your storage unit?" she asked George.

"A month to six weeks ago. It's not a place I regularly visit. I believed the word, 'security' in 'Security Storage' was truth in advertising."

"Were any of the other units robbed?"

George Melville shrugged and took another shrimp puff, then added a piece of birthday cake to his plate. "The police are checking. There wasn't any outward sign. Whoever did it didn't alter anything outside and they rearranged my belongings so if I hadn't been specifically looking for the clock I probably wouldn't have noticed it was missing."

"It sounds like a professional heist," Eve suggested. The piece of chocolate cake on her plate was intact, although the chocolate frosting had been completely removed.

"Yeah. Can't blame it on the kids this time. I'll probably never see that stuff again. *C'est la vie*, I guess."

"I heard the planning department team's run through the complete Snow to Surf course twice," Roger said. "Do you think we should do the same thing?"

"Nah," George told him. "As long as you each practice your own leg, what's the point?"

"I don't know. More team spirit?"

George patted Roger's shoulder. "You worried she's going to whip your tail?"

Roger gloomily snapped a piece of celery in two. "Yeah, I guess I am."

"Not much chance you two will be biking at the same time, Rog. There are 202 teams this year, plus four legs in front of the mountain biking. Besides, they'll be eating our dust."

"I hope so."

"Remember: winning isn't important," Ms. Moon said, balancing a piece of lemon tart on top of her full plate. "The library's sole purpose for participating in the Snow to Surf is to increase the community's awareness of reading and the library."

George and Roger thoughtfully chewed their food.

Helma folded her paper plate in half over an unfortunate cream cheese–banana concoction of Mrs. Carmon's and unobtrusively dropped it in the trash basket.

"I heard some bad news for you, Helma," Roger said.

"About what?" Helma asked as she wiped her hands on a fresh birthday napkin.

"The planning department's canoeists. They've got a line on one of those zillion-dollar Kevlar canoes. State-of-the-art job."

"What do you mean by 'they've got a line on one'?"

"Somebody south of town found them a super canoe at a really good price. You can win in one of those without even having to paddle. Still sure you want to solo the canoe leg?"

"Positive. Besides, as George said, there are 202 teams. I can't be concerned about the planning department's canoe."

"I don't know," Roger said vaguely, "if we could just beat them."

Helma returned to her desk and removed her blue spiral notebook from her purse. Beginning at page one, she read through her meticulous notes on the Joshman Lotz murder.

"Helma. Can I talk to you for a second? It's important."

It was Eve, minus her crown. She glanced pointedly at Patrice, then nodded her head toward the alcove outside the staff restrooms.

Patrice appeared to be dozing, her head bent onto her shoulder, a paper plate of food from Eve's party on her desk.

"What is it?" Helma asked Eve, moving away from the men's restroom door toward the women's.

Eve leaned against the wall and twirled a strand of hair around her finger. "I have the greatest idea and I want your opinion."

Helma waited. It was curious how often people presented inadequate information and then expected other people to fill in the blanks from thin air.

"What do you think of getting a gift for Patrice's retirement?"

"That's customary."

"No. I mean something *really* special. I know these people who are friends of a friend and they raise poodles. Purebred. What if we took up a collection and gave Patrice a brand-new little poodle puppy?" Eve ended gleefully.

Helma was uncertain. "In light of the way Patrice felt about Binky, isn't that like hoisting an orphan child on a mother whose own child has just died?"

"Is it? I could ask her."

"It would be difficult to ask without giving yourself away."

"No. I can do it subtly. But do you think it's a good idea?"

"If Patrice is ready for a new dog, I think it's a very touching idea, Eve."

"Me too."

Eve followed Helma back to her desk. Patrice was leafing through a copy of *Arizona Highways*.

"Patrice," Eve said. "Are you going to get another poodle to replace Binky?"

Helma sat down, shaking her head in dismay at Eve's "subtlety."

"Binky can never be replaced, but if I *should* ever acquire another poodle, it won't be black." Patrice said firmly.

Eve winked at Helma and left the staff room, whistling cheerily beneath her breath.

"Whistling girls and crowing hens . . ." Patrice muttered.

Helma spent the half-hour prior to her shift on the reference desk typing notes from her notebook onto her computer.

When she was finished and had printed out her results, she added a brief explanatory note to her observations, careful not to divulge any privileged information, addressed an intercity governmental mailer to Chief Wayne Gallant, and put it all into the library's mailbox.

"The detecto-bot and I are developing a relationship," Ruth said.

"You're not serious."

"Not *that* kind, Helma Zukas. Whatever are you thinking? No. He comes by, stares at me for a while; I go ask him if he wants a cup of coffee, which he declines—more politely than he used to. And sometimes he even takes me where I'm heading. And get this: he *bought* one of my paintings. I'm dying to know if he hung it in his bedroom but I doubt I'll ever discover *that*. Gives me the willies just thinking about it."

Due to the rumors regarding Ruth's involvement in murder, her show had generated so much interest she decided to drop the ill-advised plan to charge admission.

The show was a definite success. An hour into it, every painting but two sported a red "sold" dot. Helma always briefly attended Ruth's art shows to express her support of her friend even if Ruth's art left her perplexed and uneasy. It did seem to Helma that there were more attendees gawking at Ruth herself rather than her purple paintings.

Ruth in all her purple majesty had managed to wear a tragic, yet secretly joyous, face, replete with dramatic sighs and soulful glances at the door as if she might never walk through it a free woman again.

❧ chapter fifteen ❧

COTTON CANDY
INTERLUDE

The carnival rolled into town under darkness five days before the Snow to Surf Race, setting up on a spit that was visible from Helma's balcony. It was a brilliantly lit cluster of whirling colors, highlighted by the Ferris wheel pulsing with lights that switched from a giant star to blinking circles. Constellations gone mad.

Bellehaven was primed for the Snow to Surf celebration, the biggest, most anticipated festival of the year. Snow to Surf was an homage to spring, the unofficial kick-off to summer, an unspoken appeal for a season of decent weather.

There were concerts every night for a week, dances in the parks, art shows, the crowning of a Miss Snow to Surf, and a parade over which she would reign.

The first night of the carnival, Helma stood on her balcony in the darkness, lifting cans of peaches to strengthen her arms and watching the display of lights. When the traffic paused or the wind changed, a cacophony of music and screams wafted across the water, punctuated now and then by a bored voice over a loudspeaker. Boy Cat Zukas was nowhere to be seen.

"Ah, that's a sight, isn't it?"

Helma gasped. She hadn't seen Mrs. Whitney sitting on her balcony next to Helma's, also in darkness, watching the carnival.

"Hello, Mrs. Whitney. I didn't see you. Are you going to the parade on Saturday?"

"Oh yes. The senior center always reserves a section of Cartier Street a block from the reviewing stand. Maybe I'll see your mother. It's the children I enjoy watching, and all the men in those tiny cars. Are you going?"

"I'm working at the library on Saturday."

"The library should close," Mrs. Whitney asserted indignantly. "All the stores should close during the parade, too. The carnival's beautiful this year, isn't it?"

"From this distance," Helma agreed.

"Like flowers in the night," Mrs. Whitney went on. "I used to go every year. All the noise and the laughing."

"Did you take your daughters?"

Mrs. Whitney laughed. "Without them, too. The Tilt-a-Whirl was *my* ride. The way you whirled around and squeezed together, especially if you were with your sweetheart. You can have your Ferris wheel. I'd ride the Tilt-a-Whirl until I got sick if I had the chance." In the dark she chuckled again. "Now I'd probably have a heart attack."

Helma sneezed and Mrs. Whitney said, "Bless you. Are you warm enough, dear?"

"Thank you. I'm fine."

"You know what I really miss? Pink cotton candy on a paper stick. I know you can get it out at the mall but it's not the same is it?"

Another balcony door slid grittily on its tracks and the couple on the other side of Mrs. Whitney stepped out into the night. Stereo music accompanied them.

"Good night, Mrs. Whitney," Helma called softly.

"Good night, Helma."

It was only nine o'clock. Helma pulled on her light jacket and quickly left her apartment.

Traffic moved in a slow constant current near the carnival as drivers searched for a place to park. Finally, Helma did what Ruth called a "Canadian." She simply stopped in the street and waited for the next car to pull out of a space, ignoring the honking behind her.

Helma hadn't walked more than half a block toward the bright lights when she heard her name called.

It was Chief Gallant, wearing jeans and a sweatshirt, grinning his crooked grin. "I didn't expect to see you here alone, Helma," he said.

"I'm just as surprised to see you," she told him.

"I'm picking up my son. Do you mind if I walk with you?"

"Not at all."

"Are you meeting someone?" he asked. A group of teenage boys coming toward them magically parted, nodding briefly at the chief.

"No, I'm here to buy cotton candy for a friend. It should only take a few minutes."

The artificial light of the carnival flattened colors and faces until everyone looked like they were caught in a grainy video display. The machinery that spun the rides rumbled and clanked, competing with the pounding music and the noisy, wheedling barkers.

"There's a cotton candy booth by the shooting gallery," the chief shouted as they passed the bumper cars where the attendant was admonishing a man to sit down immediately or else.

Wayne Gallant stopped and faced Helma. "How about one ride with me before you buy your cotton candy?"

"I don't . . ."

"Just one. My kids wouldn't be caught dead on a ride with their dad. What do you say? Your choice." His eyes sparkled. He glanced eagerly at a strange contraption that swung riders upside down, backward, and head over heels. It made Helma dizzy to look at it.

"Ferris wheel?" he asked. "Octopus?"

The crowd jostled past them as they stood in the midway. A young girl carrying a huge teddy bear brushed against Helma, her eyes only on the boy whose hand she held.

"I think," Helma said, "perhaps the Tilt-a-Whirl."

"Good choice." His hand at her back, hovering, not touching, he guided Helma through the crowd to the whirling red ride.

Helma had never ridden on a Tilt-a-Whirl and she swallowed when she saw how the twirling seats shaped like shells spun so wildly.

"Has your investigation . . ." Helma began as they stood in line.

Wayne Gallant put a finger to his lips. "You can't talk police procedure at a carnival. It's the law."

Too quickly they were seated in the shell, the inadequate-looking safety bar snapped over their laps. Helma gripped the bar tightly, waiting with dread anticipation for the ride to begin. Wayne Gallant rested his arm on the back of the seat behind her.

With a groan, the ride began to move, slowly turning. Each shell spun on its own axis as the foundation turned beneath it. Their shell spun lazily back and forth as the foundation turned, rose, and fell. Helma relaxed. It wasn't so wild after all.

With a wrench, the shell was caught at the apex and then dropped, spinning with abandon, first one direction, then the other. Her body slammed against the chief's. She struggled to pull back but it was impossible even to lift her head from his chest. The force was just too great.

"Woo!" Wayne Gallant shouted. His arm tightened around Helma's shoulders. Colors blurred into lines, sounds were incomprehensible. She was beyond dizzy. Her hair whipped across her face. For a moment she was able to raise her head and then it was helplessly pushed back onto his shoulder.

"Excuse me," she said.

He laughed and an invisible hand pressed them together against the back of the seat. Helma felt his lips against her forehead. She clung to him, breathless, feeling she was being compressed by G-forces. His shirt buttons dug into her cheek and she squeezed her eyes closed, powerless, lost in the black gyration of movement.

But then, just as she was getting used to the twirl and lurch and spin, the Tilt-a-Whirl began to slow. The invisible hand relaxed its hold, although until the shell stopped, she didn't raise her head nor did Wayne Gallant remove his arm. Helma was exhausted.

"Okay!" the ride attendant said, pulling back the safety bar.

Helma's legs were rubbery, her equilibrium distorted, and the chief kept his arm around her until they reached the brightly lit cotton candy booth.

The round cotton candy machine inside the booth hummed, producing a few airy pink threads. Pink and blue cotton candy in plastic bags swung from hooks around the eaves of the booth.

"Two cotton candies," Wayne Gallant told the aproned man.

"Got some right here," the man said, pointing to the pink and blue display.

"Fresh," Helma requested. "On paper cones, and please carefully wrap one in plastic."

"If you say so," he said and turned on the machine.

They walked back through the crowds and lights which now seemed less oppressive than when Helma had arrived at the carnival. She cautiously protected Mrs. Whitney's cotton candy from the crush of people while she pulled a strip of pink batting from the chief's cotton candy. It melted sweetly on her tongue as if she'd imagined it.

"Thanks, Helma," he said, holding Mrs. Whitney's cotton candy while she unlocked her car door. "I enjoyed this."

"So did I," Helma agreed.

He waved to her once more as she drove past him. He was climbing behind the wheel of his car, which was illegally parked by a fire hydrant a block beyond hers.

Mrs. Whitney raised both her hands to her cheeks when she saw the cotton candy. "I'm going to eat it all right now, every bit of it. How can I ever thank you?" She laughed in delight as she painstakingly unwrapped the plastic from the bouffant pink candy. "My dear," she said. "Your eyes are certainly sparkling in this light."

It wasn't until Helma was brushing her teeth that she realized Wayne Gallant hadn't looked for his son, had in fact left the carnival without him. She removed her toothbrush from her mouth, knowing without a doubt that his son hadn't been at the carnival at all, that Wayne Gallant had followed Helma.

She rushed from her bathroom, toothbrush still in hand, and peered toward the street from the window of her back bedroom. She saw nothing but the dark night.

❧ chapter sixteen ❧

RACE DAY

Just after the gray light of dawn on the morning of the Snow to Surf Race, Helma stood on her balcony in her bathrobe and slippers, her hands wrapped around a hot cup of tea. Boy Cat Zukas, curled in his basket in the corner, opened one eye and regarded her but since neither made a threatening move, Boy Cat Zukas soon closed his eyes and curled himself into a tighter ball while Helma continued contemplating Washington Bay.

The carnival was gone, broken down sometime between its midnight closing and dawn. The spit was empty.

It had rained most of the night, a slow steady rain audible through her open bedroom window. She knew when the rain had started and stopped because she'd been awake throughout most of the night. Her mind as it headed for sleep grasped at river navigation, hidden guns, murder, and races, and intertwined them into irrational tales pulsing with threatening obstacles, misjudged currents, and terror. Each time, she'd jerked herself back to heart-pounding wakefulness, hands seeking the sides of her bed for stability, wildly searching the darkness for safe shores, greeted by the red barred numbers of her digital clock radio.

Finally, she rose from her bed and sat in her living room reading a *Library Journal* article on library budget proportioning in an ideal world, and was able to fall asleep on her couch for a good two hours before the sun rose.

It was still cloudy but Helma knew Bellehaven weather well enough to guess from the skies over Washington Bay that the day would be dry and overcast with a few sun breaks. Cool, ideal for strenuous activity.

A small sailboat passed close to the rocky shore beneath the Bayside Arms. The lone woman at the tiller raised her arm and waved. Helma waved back.

She finished her tea and went back inside her apartment, closing the sliding glass door and latching it, her mood a mixture of anticipation and dread over the approaching day's events.

Helma's phone kept interrupting her preparations.

"Helma, this is your coach," George Melville said, an unusual rasp of nervousness in his voice. "I just wanted to make sure you were up."

"I've been up for hours," Helma told him.

"Good, good. Any problems? You need help loading your canoe? Do you know where to meet? Have you got your number?"

"George, my segment of this race is completely under control. Are you on the mountain?"

"I am. I'm calling you from the pay phone at the lodge. The race begins in twenty minutes."

"I'll see you after the race."

"Right. After the race. At the finish line. Oh, here's Eve, dressed like a pink skin diver. She's cut off the bottom half of her team t-shirt. Where's your number, Eve?"

"Goodbye, George," Helma said.

"Yeah, yeah," and George was gone.

"Helma, dear," Helma's mother said when she phoned, "did you remember to pack sunscreen and aspirin? I'm wondering whether I'd see more if I watched at the bike-to-canoe hand-off or the canoe-to-mountain bike hand-off, what do you think? Dorothy wants to set up chairs along the river by the old nursery and watch you go past, have a little picnic. Which do you prefer?"

"Wherever you're most comfortable, Mother."

"Then we might go the picnic route. It'll be nearer your finish. I've already started a thermos of gin and tonics."

"Gin and tonics?"

"Stella Young taught me how to make them. They're delicious."

Before she hung up, Helma's mother said, "I know you're a fine canoeist, Wilhelmina, but be careful, please. You're my only daughter." She paused. "But if it's possible, do try to win."

Helma's 'I'd Rather Be Reading' t-shirt was still too big, although she'd washed it in hot water and put it through the dryer on high heat. It had been ordered to fit Curt, the original canoeist, and it hung nearly to the hem of her new navy blue shorts, which *had* shrunk a little when she put them through the dryer. It appeared, if she stood just right, as if the t-shirt was all she wore.

Helma pulled the shirt up and tied it in a knot at her waist. She was standing in front of her mirror, wondering if *that* might be a little risque as well, when Ruth called.

"You sure you don't want me to come along and launch you?"

"No, I need the time alone to focus my attention."

"Okay. I'll see you at the end of the canoe leg, then. Who's driving your car from one launch site to the other?"

"George Melville has it coordinated."

"Well, knock 'em dead, Helm. Break a leg. I'll be rooting for you."

And finally, as Helma prepared to carry her gear and paddles down to her Buick, she had one last call.

"Helma, this is Wayne Gallant. I just wanted to wish you good luck."

"Will you be watching the race?"

"Portions of it. Your mother called and invited me to a picnic along the river bank."

"She did?" Helma tried to amend her squawk. "I mean, did she?"

"It was nice of her but I might not make it, depending on developments here."

"Has Radio Kraft confessed yet?" Helma hastily asked, her eyes squeezed tight. Her mother . . .

"Not to his brother's murder but we're learning a few other interesting facts."

"Such as?"

Chief Gallant laughed. "We've been through this conversation before, Helma. I wouldn't concentrate on anything but the race right now if I were you. I'll see you at the finish line."

He was right and although Helma had an important question to ask him regarding the carnival, no sooner had she hung up than she forgot her phone calls, her attention completely dedicated to her responsibility to her team.

The canoe launch area was twenty miles from Bellehaven at a small park on the edge of the national forest. Helma was one of the first competitors at the site, intending to scout out the best spot from which to launch her canoe. The donut and coffee booth was still being erected; several race officials and volunteers sat at a picnic table near the first aid tent drinking coffee poured from a thermos.

Helma parked as close to the launch site as legally possible, ignoring the way her left front tire sank into the mud.

The first sound she heard as she got out of the car was the rush of moving water followed by the grumble of a motorcycle. Walter David pulled up beside her car and turned off his motorcycle, grinning.

"Thought you might like help setting up," he offered as he pulled off his helmet.

Helma was truly surprised to discover she was happy to see Walter David's clumsy figure and eager smile, glad not to be alone after all. Her concentration was skewed and she only half listened to his chatter as they untied her canoe.

"Good day for it: not too hot. Easy there."

Before the canoe was unloaded, they were surrounded by officials and citizens.

"You interested in selling?"

"My brother-in-law built a wooden canoe. It took him three years and then he didn't have the heart to put it in water. Drove around with it on top of his pickup canopy every summer for years."

"Are there any more at home like this?"

"No way I'd take a canoe like that down the river."

Helma donned her racing bib with the library's team number: 163, while the officials measured her canoe—it was well below the eighteen-and-a-half-foot limit. Then she and Walter carried it along the rocky spit, searching for an advantageous spot that wasn't too rocky or too shallow, where she could most easily and efficiently launch her canoe by herself.

"What about this?" Walter David asked when they were nearly as far downstream as the launching area covered. "It's pretty sandy and if we dig out some of these rocks, it'll be like sliding down a chute."

The sun shone down on them as they picked out the largest of the gray rocks from the site, tossing them farther up on the spit behind them. The cold, fast moving water hissed past, swirling the sand flat wherever they removed a rock.

"Are you nervous?" Walter asked.

"No," Helma answered. "Yes," she amended, "I am."

"Me too," he said.

More canoeists arrived at the park, and with them a wide array of canoes: wood and canvas, aluminum, fiberglass, high-tech Kevlar boats and bent paddles, even a canoe with high curved ends like a voyageur's canoe.

Some competitors wore neoprene booties and wet suits. Others were dressed more casually, like Helma. A changing but constant circle of admirers gathered around Helma's canoe, one of the few wooden canoes she'd seen there. She wished Uncle Tony could hear the praise for the skill they'd taken for granted all those years ago.

"It's against the rules for you to be here once the hand-offs begin," she reminded Walter David.

"I know. Once the hand-offs start, I'll keep an eye on your canoe from that grassy knoll."

"Grassy knoll?" Helma repeated, feeling suddenly cold.

"Yeah. Right over there."

A commotion at the other end of the spit caught Helma's attention. The county sheriff's black four-wheel-drive vehicle bumpily crossed the spit to the line of canoes at the water's edge, its engine groaning and official lights gyrating. Out in the water, a Zodiac holding volunteers from Search and Rescue slowly motored back and forth.

"Is somebody hurt?" a voice called and the canoeists along the spit silenced, moving toward loud voices.

"But we *paid* for it," a familiar voice protested.

"I don't care if you handed somebody a million bucks, it's *my* canoe," an angry voice responded.

The sheriff's car doors slammed and authoritative words cut off the quarreling.

"We didn't steal anything. We bought this canoe two nights ago."

Helma squeezed between two women in matching blue, craning until she saw blond Al and his blond partner from the planning department team standing beside a sleek Kevlar racing canoe: a shell so thin you could nearly see through it, sharp pointed ends to knife through the water, straight flat lines.

"Do you have a receipt?" the sheriff's deputy asked. He was tall and lean, with silver hair and moustache.

The two canoeists looked at each other. The number on both their racing bibs read 72.

"A canceled check?"

"We paid cash. He didn't give us a receipt."

"It's my canoe," the other man said. "I've got *my* papers right here."

"Who'd you buy it from?" the deputy asked Al.

"His name was Kraft. He lives in Sunspot Acres."

The man who Helma didn't doubt was the true owner said incredulously, "You bought a canoe like *this* from a guy in Sunspot Acres and expected it to be legit?"

"Listen," Al said. "Just let us do this leg of the race, okay? That's all. Then we'll deliver the canoe to you ourselves. All right?"

The true owner tightened his lips and shook his head.

"Sorry, boys," the deputy told them. "You can finish the race but I have to take the canoe."

"How can we finish the race without a canoe?" Al's partner asked.

But there was to be no more argument. Al and his partner watched helplessly as the racing canoe was pulled out of the water and loaded onto the roof rack of the deputy sheriff's vehicle.

Once the canoe had been secured and the deputy reached for the driver's door handle, Helma stepped forward. "Excuse me," she said. "My name is Helma Zukas and I'm a librarian with the Bellehaven Public Library."

"You're out of uniform," he said.

"You're not," Helma said. "That's why I'd like to speak to you regarding that canoe."

"Do you know something about it?"

Helma shook her head. "No, but Chief Gallant has information about the man who sold it to these men. I suggest you speak to the chief at once."

"Gallant," the deputy said. "That's where I've seen you. Aren't you and he . . ."

"Thank you very much for your cooperation," Helma said and headed back through the press of canoeists toward Walter David.

The crowd parted as the four-wheel-drive vehicle lurched across the gravel spit to the park grounds. Al from 72 caught up with Helma, his face tight with anger.

"Why were you talking to the deputy?" he demanded. "What do you know about this?"

"Nothing, except that if you deal with disreputable figures, you shouldn't be surprised by the consequences."

"I . . . ," he began, sputtering and red-faced.

"Excuse me," Helma said. "I have a race to run."

Finally, the crucial moments approached and crowds began gathering along the road near the hand-off line. Spectators and competitors, all in nervous good humor. A man hawked t-shirts; another twisted balloons into animal shapes for children. The theme music from the *Rocky* movies played in the background. "I'm pumped!" somebody shouted.

"Canoeists, gather round!" an official with a loud-speaker shouted, and nearly four hundred numbered contestants did just that.

Walter David stood next to Helma while the official went over the rules, which in actuality were very close to George Melville's description of, "Start at the beginning and go as fast as you can to the end."

"Just after Lomond Bridge, there's a logjam on the right, half submerged. Watch for the signs and stay left. And there's a new Y beyond Chaney Sawmill. Stick to the left channel; the right's passable but shallow."

"Look over there," Walter David whispered.

Helma did and saw Al and his partner canoeist from team 72, red-faced and rushed, carrying a green fiber-glass canoe toward the gravel spit. It was an older canoe with more rocker to it and a curved bottom.

"Where'd they get it?" Helma asked.

"There are usually a couple extra canoes around. Bet they paid top dollar to rent it for a few hours."

"First bicyclist twenty minutes out!" a voice called excitedly over the P.A. system. "Team number 35."

"Good luck, Helma," Walter said. "I'll go back by the canoes."

Helma nodded and Walter began working his way through the crowd.

"Walter?" she called after him.

"Yeah?"

"Thank you."

Walter smiled and made a thumbs-up sign.

Most of the canoeists were two-person teams. One stayed with the canoe while the other moved to the bicyclists' finish line for the passing of the wristband.

The bicyclist from team 35 zoomed into view, bent over his handlebars, spandex legs pumping, wearing a helmet shaped like a tear drop.

The canoeist from 35 raised his hand for the wristband. The exhausted bicyclist misjudged the distance and the wristband fell to the road. 35 scooped it up and raced between the orange cones that marked the path to the waiting canoes, accompanied by cheers and applause.

"I heard the runner for 91 didn't show," a man wearing number 24 to Helma's left said.

"Bummer," the canoeist next to him replied. "It's snowing up there, too. Have you heard anything about 188?"

"Nada."

After the first five teams had launched, Helma stretched out against a nearby tree, one leg straight, then the other, **arc**hing her back, listening to the calling of the numbers, the clapping and shouts of encouragement.

"Team 72. Ten minutes out!"

She shook out her shoulders, then flexed her wrists and ankles. When she finished she turned and caught another team member's eye. He winked. Miss Zukas quickly looked away, surveying the crowd, frankly surprised at the number of graying heads wearing Snow to Surf race bibs.

"Number 163 is ten minutes out!"

Helma stepped up to the official with the radio. "Would you verify number 163, please?"

"That's what I said."

"I'd appreciate a verification."

He rolled his eyes at her, spoke into the radio, listened to the crackly gibberish and then said, "You heard it. 163."

"How many teams have come through so far?"

He glanced at his clipboard. "Forty-eight."

Helma moved to the finish line, joining two other waiting canoeists and Al from team 72. Al bounced on his feet, warming up his arms, every movement over-extended, his mouth tight.

"Hey, library," he said when he saw Helma. "Are you surprised to see me?"

"No," Helma said honestly. "I'm glad you found a replacement canoe."

"I'll just bet. Your team's third, behind ours, in the local government division."

"At the moment I'd say it was too close to call."

"That'll change. Just wait. You still canoeing solo?"

"Yes, I am."

"Bad move."

Number 43 raced across the finish line to applause, successfully passing the wristband. The canoeist dashed toward the canoes, holding the band high like a trophy.

Helma straightened her racing bib, checked her life vest zipper, smoothed her t-shirt, made sure her high-top sneakers were tied with double knots, and patted Patrice's coin, which was buttoned into her shorts pocket. She flexed her knees once. Ready.

Around the curve came two bicyclists, neck in neck, heads low, pedaling fiercely.

"163 and 72!" the official announced to the crowd's cries of excitement.

Helma waited at the finish line beside 72 until the last possible instant, then she began running away from the line. Jeffrey sped toward her, his arm out.

The practice in the library paid off. Jeffrey transferred the wristband to Helma as easily as if they were still passing each other overdue book notices.

She was first, ahead of 72. She clutched the band, sprinting between the orange cones toward the spit. Spectators lining the route shouted and clapped. Behind her, at the hand-off line, she heard a sympathetic chorus of "oohs" as if a pass had been missed. She didn't look back. Her feet in the blue high-top sneakers seemed to fly.

"Helma! Helma!" Someone was puffing outside the lane. It was Walter David, red-faced. "Your canoe got moved! Thirty feet this side of where it was."

"Who?" she shouted, holding her stride.

Walter didn't answer.

"Who?" she shouted again.

"Don't know," he said, but Helma had her suspicions.

She left Walter David behind and made her rocky way across the spit, stumbling but never falling, searching frantically for the honey wood of Uncle Tony's canoe.

A woman from team 51 ran toward her, waving her arms. "It's here! It's here!" she cried, pointing to Helma's canoe.

Helma dashed toward her canoe and employed a maneuver the cousins had used as children to launch themselves onto their sleds to descend the snowy slope of Weldon Hill. She grabbed her canoe by the gunwales and pushed it and herself into the river, almost landing stomach-first on the center thwart, slapping the water with a smack, splashing, barely brushing the rocks.

Her canoe tipped but held, the bow end catching the current and turning before Helma had righted herself. She loosened her paddle from beneath the seat and dug awkwardly into the water, splashing backward but swinging the canoe straight. She began paddling down-river in long, efficient strokes, kneeling on the pad, her knees out and braced, getting her bearings.

The little canoe sped along the river's surface. Ahead of Helma, a brown canoe as thin as an arrow rounded the bend, bent paddles flashing in unison.

She dared a glance behind her. 72 was just pushing off into the river. She had a good hundred yards on them.

Then Helma firmly put the other canoes—those ahead and behind—out of her mind and concentrated on the river, its currents and eddies and obstacles. She focused on her paddling and the breeze and the position of her body and shoulders, envisioning it all as a single whole, a unit, movements orchestrated to perfection.

And in her concentration she failed to notice the spectators lining the bridges and parked beside roads as the canoeists passed beneath, didn't notice how the crowds went silent as this solo upright woman, her hardwood paddle cadently flashing, her strokes a piece of poetry and her canoe a work of art, passed by as swiftly and timelessly as a vision from a James Fenimore Cooper novel.

The canoe leg was eighteen miles long and Helma settled into a stroke just a hair's breadth below strenuous, her paddle entering and exiting the greenish water as cleanly as the body of an Olympic diver. She shifted her knees and seat to avoid tiring: knees down, then wide, heels together, leaning her hips against the seat, sitting.

She gained steadily on the canoe ahead of her, first only able to see their outline, now able to read their team number: 16.

She paddled out of a V of rapids into a narrow tunnel-like stretch of river with high dikes to protect the farmlands on either side from flooding. Slabs of concrete dumped over the banks reinforced the dikes and the vegetation was dank green, smelling of compost. It was like traveling down a trough.

"Coming up on your right," a voice cheerily called out behind her and a low straight-edged canoe zipped past her, paddled by two muscled men, shirtless except for their race bibs, their perspiring skin glowing.

"Beautiful!" the bow paddler said, nodding to Helma's canoe.

"You, too," Helma returned.

She squinted as the close river opened up into a bright sunny plain of gravel and sandbars cluttered dangerously with debris from past floods—tree trunks, stripped as clean as driftwood, roots still clinging like Medusa heads. The channel divided and Helma rose to her knees, then stood, turning her paddle for balance until she could see which river channel was faster. The right.

A volunteer with a clipboard stood next to a stream splashing into the river.

"Doin' okay?" she shouted.

"Okay!" Helma replied.

She passed one canoe, an Old Town, then a snappy yellow fiberglass canoe whose stern paddler had a cramp in his shoulder.

"Are you all right?" she asked.

"Will be," his partner said, waving a hand in thanks.

She heard the faint sound of a chase boat's motor and then it was gone around some distant bend. The river twisted back on itself, giving Helma a view first of the white slopes of the mountain and then the distant blue and white sky over the sea. Two more canoes passed her, neither of them paddling solo.

She grew aware of splashing behind her and to her right, heavy breathing like grunts. "Just so we pass her," a voice said. It wasn't necessary for Helma to turn to know that team 72 from the planning department was working furiously to gain on her position.

Helma held steady, keeping her pace, digging her paddle more deeply into the water, reaching farther, holding to the center of the main current.

A hawk flew across the water in front of the canoes and disappeared into the cottonwoods. The Nitcum River flowed through a meadow of dandelions and wild yellow broom into open farmland. 72 was nearly beside her. A Holstein cow watched contemplatively across a barbed-wire fence, chewing its cud. And just ahead, a tow-headed boy waved a flag from the yard of a blue house, shouting, "Go! Go! Go!"

Helma leaned into her strokes. There were two paddlers in 72's canoe but she was lighter and more maneuverable and she read the river currents better, taking advantage of the swiftest channels, occupying and holding the center, given an extra push by the river. Plus, she knew her canoe; they were paddling theirs for the first time.

She didn't glance into the faces of the men in the gaining fiberglass canoe. She didn't acknowledge their presence but she knew where they were, stroke for stroke.

"Up ahead," she heard the bow paddler say to the stern paddler.

Beyond the canoes, the river narrowed into thick cottonwood and alder again, bound by steep banks scoured of vegetation. She dared a peek behind her. Another canoe was visible behind them, a silhouette against farmland, but in a moment, when they entered the treed area, Helma of team 163 and the members of 72 would be alone, invisible to the other canoe and to the chase boats, behind and ahead.

Helma swallowed. A suspicion of unanticipated mischief shivered at her neck. She glanced down to be sure her life vest was zipped, then steadied herself against the seat, firming her legs and tightening her grip on her paddle.

The river turned in a smooth bend and Helma kept to the inside, swiftly carried through.

"Give over!" the bow paddler said as they entered the trees. "You're hogging the current."

Helma ignored him but unaccountably, her grip faltered and her paddle splashed an arc of water.

Team 72 reacted with unsportsmanlike words which Helma overlooked, taking the opportunity to pull slightly ahead.

"You can't win the division anyway," Al said. "The police department is in first."

"But we may be able to beat you," Helma answered calmly.

"Librarian!" he taunted her.

"You probably don't even own a library card," Helma retorted.

Team 72's bow nudged against Helma's canoe just ahead of the midsection, bumping her laterally.

Helma switched paddling sides and paddled back into the center current. "If you want this position, pass me fairly," she said. "Don't perform dangerous maneuvers."

"Get the hell over!"

Again, their canoe nudged Helma's and this time her canoe rocked precariously. Her knees slid off the pad onto bare wood. She braced herself with her paddle and regained her position but her knee pads had slid behind her.

Once again the two canoes drew neck and neck. The bow paddler dug into the water and again their canoe bumped into the bow of hers. Her canoe bucked and twisted and Helma struggled to stay upright. The little door of the bow compartment, Uncle Tony's 'lipstick holder,' swung open. Something—Helma didn't dare look down to see what it was—clattered down the floor of her canoe and into her knees. She couldn't let go of her paddle to remove it without risking her place, and it stayed there, working its way beneath her bare knees, digging into her flesh.

Helma was in danger of capsizing. Her canoe was too light, the bottom too rounded to take another hit while she still battled to regain her speed and equilibrium.

Only once, besides Lake Pointer, had she capsized and that was on Scoop River when her cousin Ricky had overturned her with a pry stroke beneath her canoe. It was vivid in Helma's memory. Very, very vivid.

Team 72's canoe came at her again and Helma remembered cousin Ricky. She saw Ricky pulling close, leaning toward her, and with a brutish pry stroke off the gunwales of his own canoe and extending out beneath hers, he'd tipped her over and gone gleefully on down Scoop River.

Helma blinked, pulling in her paddle from beneath 72's canoe, surprised. She switched sides, frantically bracing her boat, her blade flat to the water, uncertain what had happened.

Team 72's canoe rocked. Al, the stern paddler, leaned. Not realizing, the bow paddler leaned the same way and their canoe gently rolled over, pitching them into the Nitcum River.

Helma backpaddled and turned into an eddy close to

the bank. She paused long enough to wipe the perspiration from her forehead and to be sure both canoeists had their heads above water and were safely headed toward the bank.

"You're very poor sports," Helma called.

"I've had a bad day," Al called back as he grabbed for a willow branch.

Helma straightened her canoe and continued on down the river, hearing in the distance ahead of her echoing loudspeaker voices and snatches of music.

"Helma! Helma! Look here!"

Helma took in the group standing along the riverbank. Her mother waved a glass. Ruth held a sign painted in purple. "Go Helma!" it read. Chief Gallant stood beside Helma's mother, one big arm arcing the afternoon, his smile brilliant. Helma briefly raised her paddle in salute and continued on. The hand-off line was just ahead.

She glanced down and saw that of all the world's many oddities, she was kneeling on a dog's battered leash. A blue leather leash with a chewed handle and several missing rhinestones. Where had *that* come from?

Then she remembered Patrice spilling her purse in Helma's canoe. It had to be Binky's leash. Patrice had opened the little compartment. The leash had slid into the deck compartment and 72's bumping had dislodged it. And indeed, the little bow deck door still swung open. Poor Patrice.

Helma paddled furiously for the hand-off line and caught sight of Roger, wearing his tight red bicycle clothes and helmet, his mouth moving in encouragement she couldn't hear, his arms raised and waving. Behind him, her face grim, stood his ex-wife.

The crowd cheered Helma's approach. Somebody saluted with a plastic bottle of water. No, they held it out to her like an inducement.

Helma pulled ashore onto the sandy bank and leapt from her canoe. Her legs were rubbery. She nearly fell, then ran on unsteady legs toward Roger, who stood on

the very edge of the hand-off line, holding out the wristband toward him.

After Roger had safely grabbed the band and ran toward his mountain bike, Helma's exhaustion crashed
over her. She was utterly, miserably, totally drained. Her
muscles seemed to have melted away. Perspiration slid
beneath her life vest, stuck her shorts to her body. Purple
and gold lights flashed.

She leaned over, bracing her hands on her thighs,
struggling to catch her breath, trying not to vomit or
pass out.

And that's when she saw the marks on her knees from
kneeling on Binky's leash. A thin line, then a row of
round indentations, a space and two more round indentations, all from the rhinestone studded leash.

She leaned there, head down, her brain fuzzy from
fatigue, staring at the marks, puzzled. She clumsily
sorted through her memories while strangers pounded
her back and shouted something about a good leg.

When she rose, the Snow to Surf Race had receded
into the noise around her, all of it roaring like a deep
wind. She stumbled back to her canoe and pushed
through the admirers to gaze down at Binky's leash, still
on the floor of the boat.

The marks on her knees were the same pattern as on
Binky's leash, the same pattern she'd seen on Joshman
Lotz's neck.

❧ chapter seventeen ❧

FINISH LINE

"**H**elma, I'm your designated driver," Ruth said, holding the Buick's car keys in front of Helma's face. Ruth jerked her thumb behind her. "Police orders."

Wayne Gallant stood behind Ruth, holding Helma's gear bag, into which Helma had hastily stuffed Binky's leash. She stared at the bag, trying to remember how well the leash was hidden, if the chief might simply look down and see it lying there. Would he recognize its significance?

"Helm?" Ruth asked. "You okay?"

Helma raised her eyes from the gear bag to the chief's concerned face. "Just tired."

The canoe-to-mountain bicyclist hand-off area was emptying out as team members and spectators moved on to the next finish line where the mountain bikers handed off to the kayakers on the north end of the bay, and to the final finish line on the south end of Washington Bay. She couldn't recall seeing it lifted, but Helma's canoe was securely tied on top of her Buick. The chief set her bag in the backseat and held the passenger door open for her.

"Thank you," Helma said.

"I have to stop by the station and see a man about a

canoe," he told her. "but I'll meet you at the finish line. Have a good celebration. You deserve it."

"Thank you," Helma said.

Ruth turned on the engine. "Hard to believe but you've forgotten to buckle up."

"Thank you," Helma said.

Ruth turned sideways. "Helma Zukas, you are in the ozone layer. Why don't you take a nap until we get to the finish line?"

"No thank you," Helma said.

"Geesh."

Ruth steered Helma's Buick through the remaining crowd and toward the road, glancing at Helma every time the Buick jerked or wallowed on the rough track. "Get that kid out of the way," she muttered once, slamming on the brakes.

Helma closed her eyes but a nap was not a possibility. Binky's rhinestone leash filled her thoughts. She tried to formulate another possibility—any alternative to the suspicions erupting into her consciousness. But no other feasible answer emerged.

"Here," Ruth said when they were back on a paved road. "I found this on your windshield."

She handed Helma a paper napkin. Written in block letters that tore through the flimsy paper were the words, "Good job! See you at the finish. Walt."

"Who's Walt?" she asked Ruth.

"Walter David, who else? Your motorcycle buddy."

"Oh," Helma said.

"Go back to sleep."

"I wasn't asleep."

"You might as well be. God, I wish I could pass this guy. Forty-five miles per hour. Come on!"

Through her window, Helma spotted three small birds chasing a hawk above a field. The hawk rose and fell and then wheeled in the air and flapped away.

"Have you ever known a terrible secret about someone?" Helma asked Ruth.

"Dozens. Why?"

"What did you do about it?"

Ruth shrugged. "Depended on the situation. I saw a friend's husband nuzzling another woman once. I didn't tell my friend but I threatened *him* with the possibility." Ruth smiled. "You should have seen his face."

"What about a criminal secret?"

"Mmm. Let me think. I was in a store once and saw this little kid swipe a pack of baseball cards and stick them in his pocket. He headed for the door with the store dick right on his heels. I knew the dick couldn't do anything until the kid was out the door so I intercepted the kid by the gumball machines and gave him such holy hell the poor kid wet his pants—but I bet I nipped his criminal career in the bud."

Helma closed her eyes as Ruth veered into the left lane and passed two cars, her foot pushing the gas pedal to the floor.

"So what secret are you privy to?" Ruth asked.

"I'm not sure."

"Suit yourself. But speaking of secrets, can I share one?"

"If you want."

"I'm taking a little vacation in July."

"To Minneapolis?" Helma guessed.

"That's right. Three weeks worth. That ought to lay this little infatuation to rest once and for all, don't you think? Three weeks with a man who I have absolutely *nothing* in common with. We'll be lucky if we're still speaking when I leave. Hell, we'll be lucky if I last one week, let alone three."

They parked a half-mile from the final finish line and joined the stream of people heading toward the park on Washington Bay, where the race ended and the celebrations began. Folk music echoed between buildings. Jubilant voices rose in waves at what Helma guessed were the early finishers. She was grateful for the walk, for the opportunity to stretch her weary, tense muscles, to be in motion. The rhythm of her steps soothed her tumultuous thoughts.

"Want one?" Ruth asked.

"What?"

"A cheesecake sample, Helma. She's offering you a sample of cheesecake."

Helma blinked. In front of her stood a woman holding a tray of cheesecake pieces the size of checkerboard squares. Helma and Ruth were in the gauntlet of food and craft booths. Desserts and Greek pastries, tie-dyed scarves, silver jewelry, and dried flowers.

"No thank you," Helma said.

"I'll take her piece then," Ruth told the woman.

The Bellehaven Public Library's overall position in the Snow to Surf Race was seventy-fourth out of 202 teams. They'd sped into second place in the local government division, after the police department, but a satisfying twelve minutes ahead of the planning department. It was a very respectable showing.

In the midst of the festive throngs, Team 163 held its own celebration. Wearing a red t-shirt that said "Coach," George Melville beamed, standing beside a picnic table covered with food and drink. Helma's mother offered around a thermos of gin and tonics and a dish of quartered limes.

Helma sat in a lawn chair, a plate of untouched food on her lap.

Eve and Junie, eating prodigious amounts of potato chips, told and retold tales of their snowy ordeals during the downhill and cross-country ski legs.

"You're pretty quiet, Helma," Eve said when Helma declined her offer of potato chips. "Tired?"

"It's been an exhausting day."

"You did a great job. You must have paddled like a banshee to get so far ahead of the planning department's canoe team."

"Fortune was on my side," Helma said. "But it was an example of teamwork; we each did an excellent job."

"Yeah, we did," Junie agreed.

All around them, people celebrated. Musicians played, barbecues smoked, and beverages flowed. The sun shone between the clouds but Helma was cold, a cold no amount of sun could warm.

She sleepwalked through the party, smiling, graciously accepting congratulations for her small part in the race, standing with her teammates in their team t-shirts while their pictures were taken, all the time her mind on Binky's leash and the distinctive markings that were now mere shadows on her knees.

Her mind toyed with the facts, rearranging and rejecting, disbelieving, *wanting* to disbelieve. But there was no denying the marks on her knees from Binky's leash were the same as the marks on Joshman Lotz's neck.

Binky's leash lay curled at the bottom of her gear bag like a snake. And her gear bag lay on the floor of the backseat of her Buick, innocently awaiting her action.

Wayne Gallant arrived and made his way to Helma.

"I didn't have a chance to ask if you encountered any problems on the river," he asked her.

"It was crowded a few times but nothing I couldn't handle."

"Just as I expected."

Helma glanced up to see her mother avidly watching Helma and Chief Gallant chat. Her mother's cheeks were bright pink and she wagged her fingers at Helma even as she nudged her friend Dorothy to take notice of Helma's conversation with Wayne Gallant.

Ruth stood talking with Walter David, a drink in her hand, wearing his motorcycle helmet to top off her purple outfit. Walter David saw Helma looking at them and waved, his eyes moving between her and Chief Gallant.

Helma was uncertain what she and the chief were saying to one another or if her responses were even lucid. Her surroundings were a mental and physical kaleidoscope, one scene distinct before it faded into another; voices crystal clear and then reduced to garble.

"I'll go find some for you, then," the chief said, smiling and leaving her, although Helma didn't know what he was going to find for her.

Eve sat on her boyfriend's lap under a tree and Roberta and George Melville lounged on a stadium blanket on the grass, lazily talking.

Ms. Moon climbed on the picnic table and raised her arms. "Let's all give a cheer for libraries and reading!" she shouted. "Hip, hip . . ."

"Hooray," came a few scattered voices.

In the crowded park and with Helma's state of distraction, she almost missed seeing Roger's ex-wife approach Roger as he scooped three-bean salad onto a paper plate. Yet suddenly, there they were, filling her vision: dressed nearly identically: tight biking clothes and thick shoes, Connie taller than Roger, a stunningly athletic couple.

"You had a pretty good take-off," Connie said to Roger, gazing into her bottle of Gatorade.

"Your hand-off to the kayaker was smooth," Roger complimented. "Where are the kids?"

Connie waved a well-shaped arm into the crowd. "With my mom."

"You want to go biking sometime?" Roger asked.

"Maybe."

Roger deeply studied his three-bean salad. "Feel like going for a cup of coffee right now?"

"Okay."

Roger dropped his loaded paper plate into the trash can and the pair wandered off into the crush of people, toned arms touching.

Chief Gallant reappeared and handed Helma a small tube of salve. She stared at it. What was that for?

"Want me to put it on your knees?" Wayne Gallant asked.

Helma looked down. Her knees were raw with pressure burns from sliding on the bottom of her canoe. Faintly, just barely, two round indentations still showed on her left knee.

"No," she told the chief, more abruptly than she intended, afraid he'd see the incriminating marks.

"You must really be exhausted, Helma," he teased. "You haven't once asked about Radio Kraft or the Joshman Lotz investigation."

"I intend to, though."

"I'll be waiting," he told her.

The afternoon wore on and grew more remote as if Helma were inside an upturned drinking glass, able to see the socializing but unable to respond or take part.

Finally, she made her goodbyes and left, refusing both Chief Gallant and Walter David's offer to walk her to her car.

"I'd like to be alone," she said.

" 'I vant to be alone,' " Ruth intoned.

The voices receded, until they were like the happy din from a distant carnival. Helma had grown accustomed to comments from admirers of her canoe, so she wasn't surprised to see the two men standing beside her car and barely paid them any heed while she unlocked her door.

"Good race."

Helma spun around, recognizing the voice of Al, the stern paddler of team 72. Both canoeists from 72 stood beside her car.

"Really," he said, grinning. "You were damn good."

"Yeah," the other one said with less enthusiasm.

"Thank you," Helma said, refraining from returning the compliment.

"If you ever feel like company on a paddle, I'd be glad to go, Al said.

"I believe I've sufficiently experienced your paddling style," Helma said.

All the beautiful, healthy people with bright eyes and white teeth faded to invisibility as she carefully pulled into the street and joined the traffic.

She continued along the boulevard, feeling the sun through her car window on the side of her face, deeply aware of her gear bag on the floor behind her, driving unconsciously but knowing without a doubt where she was heading.

At Patrice's house she removed Binky's leash from her bag and slipped it into her shorts pocket. She didn't walk up the bowered sidewalk and knock on Patrice's front door. Instead, she skirted the fragrant front yard

and rounded the house along the flagstoned path overhung with wisteria.

Patrice sat in a wicker chair on her stone patio, surrounded by colorful blooming rhododendrons and roses.
She watched Helma enter her garden, showing no surprise, and inquired politely, "Would you like a glass of
iced tea?" motioning to the pitcher and glasses on the table beside her, as if she'd been expecting company.

Helma poured herself a glass and sat down on a
wicker chair opposite Patrice, thinking what a perfectly
romantic scene it would make, a tapestry: the gardens,
the wicker, the sunlight. If only she and Patrice were
dressed in Victorian clothing.

"Did the library team complete the race?" Patrice
asked. Her sunglasses reflected Helma's image back to
her.

Helma nodded. "We were seventy-fourth over all, second in our division."

"Congratulations. To the fleet . . ." she trailed off.

They sat silently, the only sound the clinking of ice in
their glasses. A hummingbird darted erratically past and
disappeared into the pink blossoms.

"I know why you're here," Patrice finally said in a
composed clear voice. "I've been expecting you for
weeks, knowing if anyone would figure it out, it would
be you."

"I found Binky's leash in my canoe. It must have fallen
out of your purse and jammed under the bow deck compartment."

"Binky's leash. I was a sentimental fool to carry it with
me. May I have it back?" When Helma hesitated, Patrice
chuckled softly. "Don't worry. My criminal spree has
ended."

Helma removed the leash and handed it to Patrice.
"Why did you do it, Patrice?"

Patrice coiled the leash around her hand, then held it
to her cheek as if she were cooling overly warm skin.
"Whenever it was time for his walk, off Binky trotted to

pull his leash off the wall. He'd prance around with it in his mouth until I took him out."

"Why?" Helma asked again.

"It's a long story."

Helma took a sip of tea and waited, turning slowly to view Patrice's gardens, the fresh flowers on Binky's grave. It was a sanctuary so lush that neither of the neighbors' houses were visible.

"My friend Alice was extremely naive," Patrice finally said. "Long ago, young women usually were. Everyone knew the marriage would be a disaster, but she was determined. Lotz was handsome then, before his true personality grew visible. The young believe they are the exception, don't they?

"She put the best face on it, the way women did then. But Lotz was chronically in trouble with the law and she couldn't always hide the bruises. There were rumors about why she died at her son's birth, but who knows.

"The facts were," Patrice said, "that Alice was dead and Joshman Lotz didn't want his son."

Patrice paused and swallowed. "I was newly married and we'd just moved to San Francisco. I came home when she died; she was my best friend. Catherine was eight. Plans were already in motion for the baby to be adopted out of the area."

"And Catherine?"

Patrice bowed her head and it was several moments before she spoke again. "She called me Aunt 'Trice, even though we weren't related. She begged to live with me. But I was still on my honeymoon. At the time I thought there would be children of my own." Tears slid from beneath Patrice's glasses. "That child. That beautiful little girl. She tried to tell me what her father was doing to her, but I didn't want to hear her, didn't want to believe it. I turned my back on her."

Patrice slumped, old, older than she'd been at Binky's funeral. "I'm sure I was the only one she trusted enough to tell and I abandoned her. She never forgave me and I never forgave myself. It ruined both our lives and I wasn't ever happy again. Ever," Patrice whispered. "Betrayal seeps into your heart, destroys what you touch. I didn't return to Bellehaven until shortly before she drowned. By then my marriage was over and Catherine refused to see me."

"And that's why you killed Lotz?" Helma asked. "Why wait so long? Catherine's been dead over thirty years."

"It's odd how events converge sometimes, isn't it? I heard a Ms. Moon-type term for it: synchronicity, like it's meant to be. We're carried along to an undeniable moment by events that at first glance have no relation to one another. Several events took place within a few months, weeks actually. I began to have certain symptoms and when I went to the doctor, tests confirmed that only the most drastic treatment remained, and *it* would be more debilitating than the illness.

"While I was coming to terms with that, Lotz was released from prison. I felt I had nothing to lose. I implied that Alice had sent me an incriminating letter before she died and I wanted to show it to him. Once he was here, I confronted him about Catherine. After all these years I don't know what kind of satisfaction I thought I'd gain. But I *had* to do it, can you understand? When he raised his voice, dear brave Binky came to my defense."

"And Lotz killed Binky?"

Patrice nodded. "He kicked him. Binky was too old to survive such a blow. Then Lotz threatened me and left."

"But Lotz wasn't killed until a day later and that was at Ruth's house."

"I was determined to go on, to follow my routine. Thursday night when I was returning from my lapidary club meeting I saw Lotz stumbling toward the Slope. I didn't have murder in mind. I parked my car just off the boulevard and followed him. He was drunk. The longer I followed him the angrier I grew.

"When he turned in the alley, so did I. I didn't know it was your friend Ruth's house. He stepped onto her path and stopped. I didn't stop soon enough and he heard me. That's when he turned on me. There was a board leaning against the garage. I was terrified and grabbed for it and hit him across the chest. He was inebriated and slow and it was all shockingly easy. Do you remember how we learned in the city's self-defense class to pull a jacket half off an attacker to pin his arms? I'd been carrying Binky's leash and one thing followed another. And Lotz was dead."

She faced Helma, her eyes invisible behind the sunglasses. "You wouldn't think it would be so simple to take another human's life, would you?" She held her iced tea to her mouth, wetting her lips but not drinking, before she said with conviction, "I'm not sorry. Whatever happens to me I don't regret killing him. I regret turning my back on Catherine a million times more than I could ever regret Joshman Lotz's death."

"But Ruth's been a suspect. Were you planning on allowing her to be charged with murder?"

"I knew there wasn't enough evidence. I'd have come forward if she'd actually been arrested."

Helma wondered about that. "Did you burn Ruth's garage?"

"The board was inside. That night I stood it up like it was part of the wall. But then I realized there might have been blood—or other evidence—on it. I didn't know what the police could detect from it. I didn't want to burn the garage, but the gas got away from me."

Helma finished her tea, wanting to be away from this beautiful garden and its calm, deceptive creator.

"I'd like to return this to you," Helma said, removing the good-luck coin from her shorts pocket.

Patrice took the coin and studied it. "Are you going to the police?"

"It's the proper thing to do. It's my duty."

"I'll understand if you do, Helma. My life has been dreadfully unhappy. All I've done for the past forty years is keep busy, trying not to think. To work so hard that every night I'd fall into bed too exhausted *not* to sleep. I longed to be unconscious. Maybe I could finally put all this behind me before I die."

"What's the prognosis for your illness?"

"The ending won't be pleasant. Perhaps it will be in proportion to my crimes." She laughed briefly. "I sound suitably condemned, don't I? But Dr. Freeman has assured me it will be swift. And I intend that once it begins, it will be so."

"I'm sorry, Patrice."

Patrice turned her head away. "There's no reason for *you* to be sorry, Helma. It's my own doing. My entire life has been of my own doing."

Three times Helma picked up the phone and began to dial Chief Gallant's phone number, and three times she replaced the receiver, bewildered as to why she didn't make the call. A crime had been committed and Helma knew who had committed it. Patrice had taken the law into her own hands and that was wrong. Ruth could be completely cleared, exonerated with one simple phone call.

She sat on her balcony, gazing unseeing at the lowering sun, her hands in her lap, unconsciously moving her aching shoulders to loosen them, so caught up in her thoughts that she didn't notice when Boy Cat Zukas jumped down from the balcony railing and cautiously slunk around her chair, rubbing briefly against one rear leg before he sprang back to the railing, emitting a brief volley of purrs.

Helma arrived in Chief Gallant's office without an appointment. He agreed to see her immediately and beckoned her to a chair in his office. The chief's office was more comfortable than she'd expected. She recognized paintings by a local artist. There was even a rug over the tile floor. On the table behind his desk stood a framed picture of two children, a boy with a widow's peak like the chief's and a girl with a missing front tooth.

"This time I'm blatantly requesting information," she told him. "No subterfuge. No trickery."

"If it's information I can share with you, I will."

"You didn't just happen to run into me at the carnival. You followed me, didn't you?"

Wayne Gallant placed his elbows on his desk. "Not exactly."

"Then you obviously had someone watching me and you stepped in, correct?" Helma didn't wait for him to agree. "Why?" she asked.

"Radio Kraft made open threats against you and Ruth Winthrop."

Helma sat back, suddenly seeing the truth. "You weren't just having Ruth watched because you *suspected* her, were you? You were *protecting* her."

"And you."

"What's going to happen to Radio Kraft?"

"He'll stand trial next month for breaking and entering, robbery, and trafficking in stolen goods."

"Did you recover the items I informed you of in my memo? George Melville's belongings?"

"The grandmother clock wasn't difficult to trace. Not to mention various other stolen goods. And the racing canoe he 'sold' was a pretty blatant felony."

"Very sloppy on his part. I'd guess his accomplice was involved in that transaction."

"Constantine 'Rock' Dougherty?" Chief Gallant shook his head. "A late-comer to the whole story."

"Ruth called him a dim bulb," Helma was ashamed to hear herself say. "Did Radio Kraft admit to shooting at my canoe at Lake Pointer?"

"Not yet. But if Kraft *didn't* kill Lotz . . ." The chief stopped.

"They were still brothers and he'd want revenge," Helma finished for him. "So Radio Kraft won't be charged with Lotz's murder?"

"There isn't enough evidence against him. Not enough evidence against Ruth Winthrop, either, I might add."

"She's no longer a suspect?"

"I hope she won't be disappointed."

"Being a murder suspect boosts the value of her art."

"That's what I understand." He smiled. "Detective Houston's purchase may not turn out to be the investment he thought it would be."

"So there aren't any leads on Joshman Lotz's murder?"

"Not currently." The chief raised one eyebrow. "Do *you* have any suspicions, Helma?"

Helma snapped and unsnapped her purse clasp, picturing Patrice sitting in her garden, waiting, under her own sentence. "No," she said. "I have no suspicions."

It was true; she didn't. No suspicions, only certainty.

"It was a pleasure watching you canoe," Wayne Gallant said. "You have beautiful form. Do you think that canoe would hold two people if one of them weighed about 190 pounds?"

"It might." Helma tipped her head, considering. "Yes, in fact I know it would."

A tall athletic man with graying temples approached Helma in the library, his hand out. "Miss Zukas, I'm Del Reese. I own the Sports Corral. Your canoe was one of the highlights of the Snow to Surf Race."

"Thank you."

"Would you consider letting us display it at the store? We could hang it to keep off curious hands. I can offer you a discount on your purchases at the Sports Corral in exchange."

Walter David had held off renting 1C as long as possible, but Helma knew he couldn't accommodate her much longer.

"I believe we could make arrangements beneficial to both of us," Helma told him.

Patrice's retirement party was held in the old Sam and Ella's, now under new management.

The entire staff attended, even the nonprofessionals. Patrice held court from the head of a table overhung with crepe paper streamers and a "Good Luck!" banner, wearing a dress with a definite Southwest flavor. "My sister sent it to me," she announced.

Patrice didn't say anything unusual or revealing to Helma, but once, as Helma passed her a dry tissue, Patrice squeezed Helma's hand, startling Helma so much the tissue fluttered into Patrice's salad.

"To a joyous new life," Ms. Moon said, rising and toasting Patrice with her water glass. They all rose and did likewise. "Far, far away," George Melville added softly.

Eve, who was in charge of Patrice's gift, waited until they'd all finished their "Death by Chocolate" cheesecake before she snuck out of the restaurant and returned, giggling, her smile wide, gingerly carrying a gaily wrapped package perforated with round holes. She grandly presented the box to Patrice, who took it on her lap, her face a picture of guarded wonder.

The white poodle puppy, perfectly coiffed with a pom-pom tail and pink ribbons tied to its ears, burst through the box top straight onto Patrice's bosom, wagging and wiggling and licking her neck.

"Oh, oh, oh," was all Patrice said for the longest time while they all watched the squirming puppy in Patrice's arms.

"At least we won't have to hear blow-by-blow descriptions of this one's cutesy wutesies," George Melville said as everyone clustered around the pair at the head of the table.

❧ chapter eighteen ❧

NOTHING BUT THE TRUTH

Helma removed her purse from the bottom drawer of her desk. It was quarter to two and her doctor's appointment was at two o'clock. She dreaded her annual physicals but she was as religious about scheduling them as she was about her Buick's tune-ups, one of those events she participated in "for her own good," and tried not to think about between times.

"Here's a postcard from Patrice," Eve said, handing Helma a postcard with a routing slip attached to it.

The picture was of a Spanish mission surrounded by palms. "Every day is beautiful," Patrice wrote. "Little Terry Berry has been a dear. She hardly ever barks and she minds her mommy like a good girl."

Beside George Melville's check signifying he'd read Patrice's postcard, he'd jotted in red ink, "By God. We made the old girl happy at last." Helma hoped it was true.

Roger's checkmark was absent. He was on a cruise ship in the Greek isles. It was literally a second honeymoon and no one in the library expected a postcard from him.

Helma had received a postcard from Ruth on her vacation in Minnesota, too. The picture was of a cobbled street in Minneapolis's historic section, and the brief message read, "Ten days in and we're still having a *good* time. Who can figure?"

When she lay draped with a sheet and Dr. Freeman entered the consultation room, Helma chatted about everyday things, attempting to overlay the whole undignified proceedings with normalcy.

"We had a postcard at the library today from Patrice," Helma said.

"How's she enjoying Mexico?" Dr. Freeman asked.

"She moved to Arizona."

"Is that right? I could have sworn she said Mexico. Well, I hope she's having a good time."

"She sounded like it. She told me about her tests and the prognosis you gave her."

"Waiting for test results is worse than coping with a disease, I believe."

"She seemed at peace when she left."

"She should be. It was a relief to have those tests come back negative."

"Negative?" Helma repeated, attempting to cover her confusion, glad it wasn't her face Dr. Freeman was examining. "So she has a long retirement ahead of her?"

The doctor laughed. "She'll probably bury us all. One of the healthiest specimens I've seen for a woman her age. That's why I thought she was moving to Mexico. She said the money from her house should last a lifetime and I doubt if it would here in the States. She even joked about hiring a maid."

Helma drove through two yellow lights on her way back to the library and didn't bother to line up her hood ornament with the flagpole when she parked her car.

"Eve," she asked before she'd even reached her desk. "Do you have Patrice's address in Tucson?"

"Sure. Just a minute. It's in my bag."

Helma retrieved volume one of the *American Library*

Directory from the staff shelves and sat at her desk, flipping the big blue book open to Arizona.

"Here you go," Eve said, handing Helma a *Star Wars* address book open to Patrice's new address.

"Is this her sister's phone number?"

"Mm-hmm."

Helma dialed the Arizona number, charging it to her home phone.

"Scott's Flowers," a voice answered.

Helma tried twice more and got Scott's Flowers both times.

"Maybe I wrote it down wrong," Eve said when Helma told her. "I do that thingamajig with numbers sometimes."

"Transpose them," Helma supplied.

"Right. Wait a minute. I'll get the Tucson phone book from reference."

Helma didn't expect Patrice's sister's name to be listed in the phone book, and it wasn't.

Next, Helma checked the *American Library Directory* and dialed the Tucson Public Library's reference department.

"I am a professional colleague of yours," Miss Zukas told the librarian who answered. "I'd be very grateful if you would look up a name, phone number, and address in your *Polk's City Directory*."

Eve sat on the edge of Helma's desk while they waited for the librarian to come back on line, playing with a ring on the third finger of her left hand.

The street address was nonexistent, the phone number indeed belonged to Scott's Flowers and there was no one living in Tucson with the name Patrice had given them as her sister's.

Helma closed the directory and leaned back in her desk chair. Patrice had said she'd be sharing a condominium with her "little" sister, but Helma suddenly realized that Patrice had also, in a moment's confidence on Lake Pointer, told Helma that she, Patrice, had been the last child to grow up in her family's Bellehaven home. There was no younger sister.

"That's really weird, isn't it?" Eve asked. "Do you think she got lost somewhere?"

Helma shook her head as she picked up her telephone and dialed Chief Gallant's number. "No," she told Eve, picturing a tanned, ramrod woman with champagne hair seated in a lounge chair in a tropical southern climate, wearing sunglasses, drinking an iced drink with her adoring and adored poodle by her side. "I think Patrice is exactly where she intended to be all along."